Dark Days at Drumshee

Book 12 of the
Drumshee Timeline Series

D0806268

Cora Harrison taught primary school children in England for twenty-five years before moving to a small farm in Kilfenora, Co. Clare. The farm includes an Iron Age fort, with the remains of a small castle inside it, and the mysterious atmosphere of this ancient place gave Cora the idea for a series of historical novels tracing the survival of the ringfort through the centuries.

Other books in the Drumshee Timeline Series

Dark Days at Drumshee

CORA HARRISON

WOLFHOUND PRESS

VAN COUNTY LIBRARY

C. No. ..C/1.26188..
J
ASS No. ......J...........
OICE NO. 2052 IES.
CE........E.6.:.03...

Published in 2002 by

WOLFHOUND PRESS
an imprint of Merlin Publishing
16 Upper Pembroke Street
Dublin 2
Ireland

www.merlin-publishing.com

Text Copyright © Cora Harrison 2002
Cover and Internal Illustrations © Albert Jackson 2002
Author's Photograph © Mike Mulcaire 2002

ISBN 1–903582–32–6

All characters and events and places referred to in the book are fictitious
and are not intended to refer to any person living or dead.
Any such reference is coincidental and unintentional.

A CIP catalogue record for this book is available from the British Library.

All rights reserved. No part of this publication may be reproduced,
transmitted, or stored in a retrieval system of any kind without
the permission of the publisher.

Cover Design by Pierce Design, Dublin
Typeset by Carrigboy Typesetting Services, Cork
Printed by Cox and Wyman Limited, Reading

For Clare Silke of Barna, Galway,
who not only named Silky, but also brought
the pony to life with her vivid imagination
and wonderful descriptions.

Cavan County Library
Withdrawn Stock

Chapter One

'If, by chance, Conor O'Brien were to be killed, we'd have an easy victory,' said the first voice softly.

'Wise men leave nothing to chance,' said the second voice, a strange, metallic voice. 'We must make sure that he is killed.'

Alys shivered. These were dark and dangerous days, but to hear murder plotted — the murder of a man whose lovely children she had just left playing happily around their mother . . . that sent an icy chill over her whole body. She stayed very still, thankful that the thick hedge hid her from the men.

There were three of them, she reckoned. She had heard the clip-clop of their horses' hooves coming down the road, and she had hidden behind the hedge — in these troubled times, any stranger might be an enemy.

Then there had been a sudden startled shout from a young, light voice, and the other two horsemen had stopped, just opposite her hiding-place. All she could see, in the dusk of the late-autumn evening, was the gleam of silver from their armour.

'That's all right now,' said the young voice. 'I've taken the stone out of his hoof. No harm done. We can ride on.'

'Those are the lights of Lemeanah Castle ahead of us,' said the first man. He had an English accent; they were all three English, Alys guessed. 'I've heard it's a splendid place. Conor O'Brien built a fine new house onto his castle a couple of years ago. We should be comfortable there. There'll be room for the men, too, once they arrive. They should be there in an hour or so – that's plenty of time to make sure everything's ready for them. They'll appreciate some comfort; it's a long march from Kilkenny.'

Comfortable? Alys could not understand. One minute they were plotting murder, and the next they were talking about the comfort of their victim's house. Could she warn the household – put them on their guard? Could she get back to Lemeanah Castle before the men reached it?

They had moved on. There was a chance that they would see her if they looked over their shoulders – the road was straight – but she dared not risk any delay. She had to reach Lemeanah before they did. She had to warn Máire Rua that her husband was in danger. Without

giving herself the chance to feel afraid, Alys plunged through the thick hedge, rapidly crossed the road – it was empty; the riders had made good progress – gathered up her long skirt in one hand, neatly vaulted the low wall and raced across the fields to Lemeanah Castle.

She was too late, though. By the time she arrived, the studded oak front door of the castle had been thrown open and there was Máire Rua, splendid in her floor-length purple satin dress, with the light from the torches glistening on the snowy white of her lace collar. And she was welcoming the three horsemen! Welcoming them, holding her hands out to them, calling the children to come and greet them!

From behind the small gatehouse, Alys watched. She couldn't see the three men – they had their backs to her – but she could see the children. There was Donogh, only nine years old, but so grown-up that he too was making a little speech of welcome. Teige and Torlach were shyer – they were hanging back. Honora, busily making sure that the light fell on her diamond ring, which had been left to her by her grandmother; Mary, beside her, smiling prettily; Slaney, in her mother's arms – they were all being patted and kissed by the three strangers.

Alys examined the men carefully. She couldn't see their faces, but she could see their clothes and their outlines. Two of the men were middle-aged, she thought, but the third was not much more than a boy; his voice had sounded young when he had shouted on the road, and from the back he looked young and slim. The men were English; but they were not Cromwellians. They were dressed as Cavaliers, with long hair, and fine lace at their wrists and throats.

The English Cavaliers, the Royalists, were still loyal to the murdered King Charles and to his son, who had been crowned Charles II by the Scots; and they were fighting on the same side as the Irish, against the followers of Oliver Cromwell. The English Royalists and the Irish were Confederates – they were all part of the same army, fighting to put Charles II on the English throne. The terrible massacre at Drogheda had shown them all what they could expect from the Cromwellians. So why should these Cavaliers plan to murder Conor O'Brien, who was the leader of the Irish here in Clare and an important man in the Confederation of Kilkenny?

Alys shrank back into the shadow of the wall. Máire Rua must know who they are, she thought; she must be expecting them. If I say anything, I'll just look silly. Worse still, I might be turned out of the house before I even start working there. . . . Quietly she turned and slipped away, back through the vegetable garden, across the roads and through the fields, back to Drumshee.

Chapter Two

Grace McMahon, who had once been Grace Barry of Drumshee Castle, sat by the fire in the little cottage that her husband, Enda, had built for her more than sixty years ago. Enda was dead – he had been dead for ten years, and she had missed him every hour of those ten years. She was seventy-seven, and she had begun to live more in the past than in the present. What a happy life we had, Enda and I, she thought. And what good children!

Cecilia, the pretty one, had made a fine marriage over in England. She had gone to live there with her godmother, Grace's cousin Judith, when she was fourteen years old; a knight from Kent had fallen in love with her, and they had married. I haven't heard from Cecilia for years, thought Grace sadly. Her eldest boy, Charles, must be over forty now. . . . And then there was Maeve, clever

Maeve: she was the Reverend Mother at the convent in Kilshanny. And tomboy Bridget was the wife of a farmer over near Inchicronan, half a day's ride to the east of Drumshee; she had a big family, so she didn't come to see her mother too often. Brendan, Conor and Declan had gone overseas – they were soldiers in Spain. Only Niall was left, out of them all.

Still, thought Grace, I'm a lucky woman. Niall is a good son, and his wife Betty is kind to me. And there are my grandchildren. . . . Baby Owen was in the cradle at her feet, Eliza was nine years old, Dermot was twelve and out helping Niall with the cows – and then there was Alys, fourteen years old and her grandmother's favourite.

At the thought of Alys, Grace suddenly felt cheerful; she bustled about the kitchen, putting a cloth on the big table under the window, taking down silver-grey pewter goblets from the dresser that Enda had made so long ago, swinging the iron crane over the fire so that the blackened kettle hanging from it would boil. Alys would soon be home, and she would need a hot drink after her long walk through the cold, wet fields.

'She's coming,' shouted Eliza from the door; but Grace had already heard the neighing of the ponies in the Togher Field. The ponies – all of them descended from Grace's own pet pony, Golden Dawn – loved Alys more than anyone else on the farm.

'I've got it, Granny!' And Alys was in the room, her hazel eyes glowing, her black ringlets damp from the mist and her cheeks pink from the cold.

'You're going to be the nursemaid at Lemeanah Castle!' shrieked Eliza. She ran out into the yard, shouting, 'Mother, Father, Alys is back! She's got it!'

'Did you see them all?' asked Grace. 'Was Conor O'Brien there?'

Alys shook her head. 'No, just the children and their mother, Máire Rua. Conor O'Brien wasn't there.' Her face clouded at the thought of the words she had heard on the road.

'He's probably off fighting,' said Betty, her mother, coming in through the door from the haggard. 'I heard that he's the High Sheriff of County Clare now. They're fighting Cromwell's army. There's going to be bad trouble soon. I wonder how long it'll be before the fighting spreads up here.'

'It's a lovely place, Lemeanah,' said Alys. 'The new house that's built onto the old castle is full of beautiful furniture. The walls are all panelled with wood, with pictures hanging on them.' She didn't want to talk about war or trouble. She wanted to enjoy the excitement of growing up and earning money for the first time in her life.

'So you saw Máire Rua, then,' said Grace thoughtfully. 'What's she like? Were you afraid of her?'

'No,' said Alys slowly. 'I think I might be if she were angry, though. She has a fierce look about her.'

Grace chuckled. 'She's a fierce lady, all right,' she said. 'Did you ever hear tell of how she rode out with her husband and his brothers and friends one night, a few years ago, and they drove all the English settlers out of Inchovea Castle and all the other places around here? That was the beginning of the Plantations in this part of Clare – and it was the end, too! Even Cromwell and his men haven't dared plant Englishmen in North Clare since then. She's a very brave woman, Máire Rua. And she was only just after getting out of her bed after her eldest was born.'

'That must have been about nine years ago, then,' said Alys. 'Donogh is nine years old. Teige is eight, Torlach is seven, Honora is five, Mary is four and Slaney is three. I have to look after them all. The little ones are sweet, but I'm not sure about the boys.'

'Well, you manage to get Dermot to do what you want, and he's older than those three,' said her mother.

'No, she doesn't,' said Dermot, coming in with his father.

'Donogh,' said Grace. 'That's the little fellow that had the plague when he was only two months old. Máire Rua was lucky to save him – but she's a strong woman herself; the boy probably took after her. It's not many babies that recover from the plague. I know you did, Alys, you and Dermot; but then, you were older when you got it. I knew the boy's great-great-grandfather – he was called Donogh as well; he used to come here to dinner. That was in the days of Drumshee Castle, of course. I was only a girl then.'

'You can't forget the days of your grandeur, Mother,' teased Niall, kissing Alys. 'So you're off to work, then,' he said affectionately. 'Good girl. That'll be a nice start in life for you.'

'I've been thinking about Drumshee Castle recently,' said Grace, following her own thoughts, as old people do. 'I don't know why, though. It was blown to a heap of stones by a cannon, before any of you were born. It was in the year of the Spanish Armada, and that was sixty-three years ago.'

'Will they board you at Lemeanah?' asked Betty.

'They did offer,' said Alys hesitantly. 'Máire Rua showed me my room.' She stopped for a moment, remembering the little bare room at the very top of the castle. It was as well furnished as her own room, under the thatch in the cottage at Drumshee, but it seemed bleak and cold in comparison. And then there was her family — little Owen, Eliza, Dermot, her parents, her grandmother. . . . She had made up her mind instantly when she had thought of her family.

'I told her that I'd really prefer to live at home,' she said firmly. 'I can easily walk across the fields.'

Her mother frowned. 'That would be a long walk twice a day,' she said. 'It would take you nearly an hour, and the fields will be wet every day from now on. The weather will be bad with the winter coming; the dark days are here already. You'd be better off boarding there.'

'I don't mind getting wet,' argued Alys. 'I never catch cold.'

'You'd best do what your mother says,' said Niall. 'It would make sense to stay there, you know.'

'She could have Golden Silk,' put in Grace. 'After all, she did all the work of training that pony. If she had Golden Silk, she'd be over and back in a flash and she wouldn't get her feet wet.'

Alys caught her breath with excitement. Golden Silk – Silky, Alys always called her – was the most beautiful of all the ponies. She was just two years old, pale gold with an even paler gold mane, an elegant head and soft brown eyes; she was very gentle, yet inquisitive and high-spirited. Alys loved her intensely. Could it really be true that she would have her for her own?

She looked at her father and mother, saw the doubt in their eyes, and resolutely put the thought out of her mind. Golden Silk was due to be sold. She was so beautiful that they would get a high price for her, and the money was needed at Drumshee.

'I'll be all right, Granny,' she said quickly. 'I can walk easily. We'll need to sell Golden Silk now that she's trained.'

'I say she should have Golden Silk,' repeated Grace stubbornly. 'She deserves something for all the work she puts in with the ponies.'

Niall looked at Betty, who shrugged her shoulders. 'Well, the ponies are yours, Mother,' she said, trying to control the irritation in her voice.

'I'll walk,' repeated Alys.

Betty laughed. 'You're a stubborn pair, you and your grandmother,' she said affectionately. 'But she's the oldest, so she's the most stubborn. You'd better take the filly.'

'I can buy her,' said Alys, with a great blaze of excitement warming her. 'I'll be getting sixpence a week from Máire Rua.'

'No need for that,' said Niall hurriedly, with an eye on his mother. 'We can manage. I never count on a pony until it's sold. Too much can happen to them.'

'We'll take threepence a week,' said Betty decisively. 'Alys is right. She's a woman of means now; she can afford a pony.'

That's even better, thought Alys. This way I don't need to feel guilty or worried about it. 'A woman of means!' She liked the thought of that.

'Thanks,' she mumbled, looking around at them all. 'Thanks very much. I'll just go and see Silky and tell her the news.'

Without waiting for a word, she rushed out the door, jumped the stone wall, and ran through the cabbage garden and down to the Togher Field. The ponies all began neighing when they heard her voice, but she had eyes for only one of them.

'Silky – oh, my darling Silky,' she was calling as she ran towards the beautiful blond pony. They met in the middle of the hilly field, and Silky's soft lips nuzzled at Alys's neck. Alys gazed into the gentle brown eyes and rubbed the bristly nose.

'I'm a woman of means, Silky,' she whispered. 'I own you now. You're my very, very own.'

She placed both hands on Silky's back and vaulted onto the pony. Silky had neither halter nor saddle on, but Alys did not care; she was such a good rider that she often rode bareback, though she had trained Silky to wear a saddle. Now her feelings of excitement were fizzing inside her; she just wanted to ride instantly, and to ride like the wind. Swiftly she clapped her knees to the young pony's sides. 'Trot, Silky, trot,' she whispered, and gently turned Silky's head towards the avenue.

They trotted down the avenue that led from the cottage to the gate, then crossed the lane and went into the Big Meadow. Here Alys had set up some jumps, using haycocks and pieces of wood, and she schooled the horses every day. Normally she tacked up the horses before she jumped with them, but today she didn't care. Silky would not let her down. Holding the silvery-blond mane, she rose into the air – a perfect jump! Around and around the field they went; then they set off back up the lane, through the Togher Field, towards the *cathair*, the ancient fort that crowned the top of the hill at Drumshee.

When they reached the little Cathaireen Field beside the fort, Alys stopped to let Silky draw breath. To the northeast, across the fields, she could see the top of Lemeanah Castle. The old tower, and the new house beside it, showed black against the sky. For a moment, her worry about the three men and their plan came back to her; but she shook her head to clear the thought out of it.

'Come on, Silky,' she said aloud. 'Let's get you into the stable, and then you can have a nice feed of oats. We're both starting work tomorrow.'

Chapter Three

'Hallowe'en today,' said Grace, when Alys came into the kitchen the next morning. 'Take care of yourself on the way to Lemeanah. I remember Deirdre, my aunt's cook, used to say that there were ghosts around the roads on Hallowe'en.'

Better ghosts than men with murderous plans, thought Alys; but she smiled at her grandmother, took her platter of porridge and sat down between Dermot and Eliza.

'There's going to be a Hallowe'en party at Lemeanah Castle tonight,' she said to her mother. 'The children will all be allowed to stay up late, so I promised Máire Rua that I'd stay the night. Silky can stay in the stables there. They have lots of horses and ponies; she won't be lonely.'

'We won't see you for a couple of days, then,' said Betty. She said no more, and Alys was grateful. Her mother was right, she supposed: it would probably make more sense for her to board permanently at Lemeanah Castle – but somehow she didn't want to do it.

'I'm going to be lonely without you,' said Eliza suddenly.

'I'll see if I can bring you home some food from the party,' promised Alys, swallowing the last of her porridge and getting up hastily from the table.

'She looks nice and neat, with her new dress,' observed Grace, examining Alys. 'She'll need something to cover her hair, though.'

'I've got a linen coif in my bag,' said Alys, shaking back her black ringlets and looking down at the long dress of cream-coloured linen that Máire Rua had given her the day before. 'I'll put it on when I get there. It might fall off while I'm riding.'

Quickly she put her old red woollen cloak over her dress. She wished that she had a new cloak, or else that she could go without one; but it was a cold, misty morning, and in any case the cloak would protect her dress from mud-splashes.

'Goodbye, everyone,' she said hastily, as she took down her saddle from its nail above the fireplace – the saddle had cost a lot of money, and Alys kept it there to keep it dry and safe. She waved her hand and walked quickly out of the door. Funnily enough, she almost felt as if tears were coming into her eyes.

She ran down the avenue, picking a small apple as she went, and into the Togher Field. She always loved to see the ponies in the field in the misty early morning, when they were grazing or, sometimes, just standing very still and looking around. They all lifted their heads when they heard Alys coming, and Silky came trotting over as if she knew what was happening.

'First day at work, Silky,' said Alys, holding out the apple. Silky's soft lips just touched her hand as she delicately took the apple between her strong white teeth. She stood quite still, chewing the apple, while Alys buckled on the saddle and checked the girths.

It was still early in the morning, and Alys met no one as she cantered across the fields; but just as she was coming down the hill towards the road, she heard voices shouting commands. Quickly she reined in Silky and stood there, waiting just behind the hedge, where she couldn't be seen.

Around a bend in the road – just where she had seen the three Englishmen the day before – came a company of marching men, all dressed in helmets and leather jerkins and heavy boots. Three men rode at the head of the column, but Alys was not sure whether they were the men she had seen the evening before. It had been getting late then, and the weather had been foggy; she had never really seen their faces – just shapes in the dim light.

Hesitantly she moved forward, but she waited at the bottom of the hill until the long line of marching men had gone on down the road towards Lemeanah.

'Come on, Silky, trot,' she whispered, when she could no longer hear the footsteps ringing against the stones of the road.

The words had barely passed her lips when Silky shot forward. In a minute they had almost caught up with the company. Alys pulled Silky to a halt again and watched while the soldiers marched through the Lemeanah gatehouse, around to the barns behind the castle. The three men on horseback, however, dismounted and went up the castle steps, through the open front door. The door was shut almost immediately – but not before Alys glimpsed the mistress of the house coming forward and embracing one of the men.

That must be Conor O'Brien, thought Alys. So those three must be the men I saw yesterday – and I must have misheard them. In fact, when she thought about it, she wasn't at all sure what the first man had really said. She had heard the second man's words very clearly, but the first man's voice had been very soft. The name he had mentioned might not have been Conor O'Brien at all.

Thoughtfully Alys dismounted and led Silky around to the stables. There was no one there – all of the stablemen were busy in the big barn, laying down beds of hay for the soldiers – so she rubbed down Silky herself, and hung her precious leather saddle on one of the nails. Then she went into the kitchen.

The kitchen was huge. Its floor was made of stone slabs, which had been cut from the Cliffs of Moher, seven miles away, and brought to the castle on carts. In the middle of the floor was an enormous oak table, with benches and stools around it. On the table were wooden platters, heaped with hunks of bread and cheese, and about forty goblets already filled with ale. Obviously the kitchen had been ransacked to feed the soldiers.

'I see you have company,' said Alys to the red-faced woman who was bending over the huge fire in the hearth.

'Oh, Alys, there you are,' said Bridie, busily pouring water from a blackened kettle into the vast iron pot that hung over the fire. 'There are lots of English soldiers and officers here — friends of the master. They came back from Kilkenny last night — they've all been out marching already this morning. And now the master's arrived as well; met them on the road, he did. The mistress says for you to go straight up to the hall. The children are with her.'

So that's who it was, thought Alys, feeling a wave of relief that she had said nothing last night. Friends of the master. They're on our side. I must have misheard them after all.

Aloud, she said, 'I'll go up now. Do I look tidy enough?'

'Let me put your coif straight. God bless you, you have lovely curls; it's a shame to cover them up. There, I'll just set it back a little. Tie on this apron so that the children don't dirty your dress. If I know that lot, they'll be pulling and dragging at you all day long.'

Alys tiptoed up the grand staircase to the great hall above. She could hear the sound of voices: the deep tones of older men, a fresh younger voice, the shrill treble tones of the children, Máire Rua's quick, incisive speech. They were all talking English, and Alys was thankful that her grandmother had always spoken English to her since she was a young child. Timidly she pushed the door open and entered the hall.

It was a magnificent room. One wall was filled by three large stone-mullioned windows; the others were panelled in oak. Although the morning was dark, the room was as bright as noon: from the oak ceiling hung six great iron hoops, each of them bearing two dozen white candles. At the end of the room was a carved stone fireplace glowing with burning logs, and beside it stood Máire Rua and the three men whom Alys had seen earlier.

'It's Alys!' shrieked Honora, and Mary and Slaney ran forward to seize her hands and drag her over to the fireplace.

'Come and greet my father,' said Donogh, in his grown-up way. 'Father, this is Alys McMahon. She is going to look after the younger children for Mother.'

He sounds as if he's nineteen, not nine, thought Alys, not knowing whether she felt amused or irritated.

'Good morning, sir,' she said, and curtsied. She felt a little nervous, but Conor O'Brien looked kind. He had an open, good-natured face.

'You speak English?' he asked.

'Alys speaks very good English,' said Máire Rua. 'That's why I chose her. I want the children to grow up speaking English, Colonel Roberts,' she added, turning to an ugly middle-aged man with a very long nose. 'Alys's grandmother taught her.'

'And taught her beautifully, I am sure,' said Colonel Roberts in a bored tone. 'And now, if you'll excuse me, I'll just see to my men.'

'So you're from Drumshee, then,' said Conor in a friendly way, as Colonel Roberts left the room. 'Your grandmother is Grace McMahon, isn't she? Well, Sir Charles, this must be a cousin of yours, if Grace McMahon is your grandmother also.'

Alys looked at Sir Charles with astonishment. He seemed a very fine gentleman, and definitely English.

'I'm the son of your Aunt Cecilia, Grace's eldest daughter,' he informed her. 'My father was Sir Charles Cunningham, and my name is Charles as well. My mother asked me to visit her mother when I was over here. I have brought letters and gifts. If you will permit me, I will go home with you tomorrow and meet your grandmother and your father, my uncle.'

'She'll be pleased to see you,' said Alys happily. 'She's always talking about Cecilia and wondering how she is.' This man can't be the one who spoke those words, she thought. This is my own cousin. He wouldn't plan murder.

'And this is my stepson, Francis Chandler,' Sir Charles was saying, beckoning forward the young man. 'He is my wife's son from her first marriage.'

Alys curtsied again. Her eyes widened. Francis was one of the best-looking young men she had ever seen. He had brown eyes, and his long curly hair was the colour of late-summer corn. He wore the beginnings of a small, pointed beard and a well-trimmed moustache, and he was dressed in dark-blue broadcloth and the finest lace.

'May I be a cousin, too?' he asked gaily, planting a kiss on Alys's cheek. She blushed and stole a half-glance under her eyelashes at Máire Rua, but the lady of the house was just smiling genially.

'You can come with me tomorrow, Francis, and meet the rest of your cousins,' promised Sir Charles.

'We're all going out to the orchard,' said Donogh, still in his most lordly manner. Alys noticed that he wore a small sword by his side – a present from his father, no doubt. 'We're going to gather apples for the apple-bobbing tonight.'

'And some turnips to carve into ghosts' heads,' said Teige eagerly, producing his knife from his belt.

'I'll come too,' said Francis. 'I'm good at ghosts. And I've got a good knife.' Quickly he produced a wicked-looking knife from his own belt.

'The two little ones had better not go out into the orchard,' said Máire Rua. 'They'll only get their feet wet. Leave them in the kitchen with Bridie, Alys.'

Mary and Slaney were not very pleased to be left in the kitchen, but Alys, once she had found some baskets for the apples, promised that everyone would be back soon and then shut the door on them. She was glad that Francis was coming. Teige and Torlach were waving their knives around dangerously, and Donogh kept drawing his sword in and out of the miniature scabbard that hung from his belt.

'I'm very good at climbing trees,' said Honora proudly, just as Alys was thinking that she, at least, would be no trouble. 'Watch me, Alys.'

Before Alys could stop her, she had bunched up her long skirt in one hand, caught hold of a low branch with the other, and started to climb up the slippery, mossy trunk of the nearest apple tree. Her lace-edged petticoat showed white for a moment and then became streaked with green. There was an ominous tearing sound as a broken branch ripped the skirt of her grey dress.

'Honora, come down,' said Alys in horror.

'It's only my old dress,' said Honora unconcernedly. 'I have a pretty blue one for tonight. Catch!' She threw down some apples, and Alys quickly picked them up and put them in a basket.

'Down you come,' said Francis, catching Honora by the waist and swinging her down to the ground. 'I can pick the rest. You're too pretty a lady to be picking apples.'

'Am I?' said Honora, looking quite pleased with herself. 'Look, Francis, there are some lovely red ones over there.'

Francis picked the apples and then took the boys over to the turnip heap, where they each selected a turnip to carve.

'It's starting to rain,' said Donogh, with an anxious glance at his beautiful outfit and his gleaming sword. 'Let's go into the kitchen and carve the turnips there.'

'You'll come too, Francis?' asked Teige

'I'll have to,' said Francis seriously. 'I'm afraid of Donogh's sword. If I don't do what I'm told, he might stick it into me.'

Alys laughed, but she was pleased that he was coming.

The kitchen was warm and cosy, with the roaring fire, and Bridie was making apple cakes at the table. The room was suspiciously quiet, though. Alys gave a quick glance around.

'Oh, Bridie, where are Mary and Slaney?' she asked.

Bridie gave a guilty start. 'Aren't they there? They must have followed Macha out into the barn. Run out, Alys. They've probably gone to see the men. I was busy with the apples.'

Alys ran out into the yard. Most of the men were there, near the door, where a makeshift kitchen had been set up – a big pot of meat and vegetables, on a stand over a fire. There was no sign of Mary and Slaney.

'Have you seen two little girls?' she asked one of the men.

'They're in there, in the barn,' he said, jerking his thumb. 'One of the lads isn't well, and they're playing nursemaid to him.'

Alys hurried into the barn. It was almost dark; there was just one covered lantern beside a stall. Two men – officers, she guessed from their fine clothes – were standing beside it. Their backs were turned to her, but as she passed she heard the whisper – just four words:

' . . . The victory at Drogheda,' said one man; and immediately the other said, 'Shh!'

Mary and Slaney were down at the far end of the barn, where piles of hay had been made into rough beds for the men. Mary was holding a pewter goblet to a man's lips and Slaney was sitting beside her.

'Poor man, he sick,' said Slaney.

'We're his nurses,' said Mary, pouring some water into the man's mouth and spilling most of it on the hay.

'I've got such a headache,' groaned the man.

'I'll send someone to you,' promised Alys. A feeling of panic came over her. Soldiers from England often brought disease with them; she knew that. 'Come on, children. All the others are in the kitchen; they're carving the turnips to make funny heads.'

She caught Mary and Slaney by the hands and pulled them out into the yard. 'Someone had better see to that man in there,' she said curtly to the crowd around the fire. She dragged Mary and Slaney over to the well and quickly pulled up a bucket of water.

'I'll just wash your hands and faces before you go in,' she said. Her mother was good with sicknesses, and she always believed that washing helped to keep away fevers. Alys wished that Betty were with her. She would probably rush out to her herb garden and make the two little girls something to drink that would keep them safe.

'Come on,' she said, as she dried their hands and faces with her new linen handkerchief. 'Let's go into the kitchen. It's nice and warm there.' Probably there's nothing much wrong with the man, she thought, trying to push her fears from her mind. He might be just tired after the long march from Kilkenny.

She opened the door to the kitchen. The whole room smelled of apples and raw turnips. At one end of the table, Francis and the three boys were busily carving out eyes and noses and mouths from the hollowed-out turnips and placing candle-ends inside them. At the other end, Bridie was helping Honora to tie long pieces of string to the apples and then hang them from the clothes-drying rack that swung from the ceiling.

Alys set Mary and Slaney to work picking out small red apples to float in basins of water for the apple-bobbing, and she herself helped Honora by piercing the holes in the apples so that Honora could pass the string through them. Everyone in the kitchen was quiet and busy.

It was only then that Alys remembered the words she had heard in the darkness of the barn.

'The victory at Drogheda,' one of the unseen men had said; and the other had said, 'Shh.'

But the battle at Drogheda had been a victory only for the Cromwellians; for the Irish and the Royalists it had been a defeat, a massacre. No Irishman, no Englishman loyal to the king, would call it a victory.

Who were those men in the barn who had spoken of Drogheda like that?

Chapter Four

At about four o'clock all of the children, except Donogh, went to have a rest.

'They'll be up till all hours, so they'd better rest until the visitors arrive,' said Máire Rua to Alys. 'Have an hour off, and go up and dress them at about half past five. Then tonight they can enjoy themselves for as long as they can keep their eyes open.'

The children's rooms were on the third floor of the house, up under the roof, with the servants' bedrooms. Alys was glad to see that there were bars across the windows of the boys' room, as well as those of the little girls' room. Teige and Torlach were the wildest children she had ever known. She left them wrestling on the floor like a pair of puppies and went into the girls' room.

Mary and Slaney were sleepy, but Honora demanded a story. Alys dug deep into her memory and told the story of how her grandmother Grace had gone to the court of Queen Elizabeth, nearly seventy years before. Honora was deeply interested in all the gowns that Grace had worn, and Alys had to go on and on inventing details. It was quite a while before Honora's eyes began to droop and her long, regular breaths told Alys that she was asleep.

Now for those boys, she thought as she went back down the passageway. Let's hope they haven't killed themselves in the meantime.

She had a surprise when she opened the door. The room was very quiet; Teige and Torlach lay meekly in bed, with their blankets drawn up to their chins, and sitting on the end of Torlach's bed was Francis.

'Now remember,' he said firmly. 'No sleep now, no riding tomorrow.'

With these words, he got up, beckoned to Alys and went out with her, closing the door behind him. For a moment they both stood outside the door, listening; but there was not a sound from either of the boys. Francis beckoned to Alys again, and they both stole away down the passageway.

'They're a spoilt pair; you'll have your work cut out with those two,' Francis said as they went down the stairs together. 'I've promised to take them riding tomorrow.'

'I'll remember about the riding,' said Alys thoughtfully. 'I've got my pony here. I could teach them.'

'You're a good rider, then?' he asked, with a note of amusement in his voice.

'Yes,' said Alys firmly. She had never felt like this before. She was excited and glowing all over, and she wanted to impress Francis more than she wanted anything else in the world. 'Do you want to see me ride?' she challenged.

'Yes,' he answered, and gave a warm smile that made her heart beat faster than ever.

The men were still lounging around in the yard, roasting apples over the blazing fire. Alys peered quickly into the dark barn, but there was no sign of the sick man. Perhaps he was feeling better. Maybe he was just tired, she thought.

'Here's Golden Silk, my pony – I call her Silky,' she said as she led the way into the stables.

'She's a beauty,' said Francis, his brown eyes wide with delight.

'You can stroke her,' said Alys, taking down her saddle and starting to tack up Silky. 'She's as gentle as a lamb.'

'If you want to ride her, you can take her out in the trotting lane,' said Michael, one of the stablemen, over his shoulder. 'Look, it's out there, to the north of the stableyard. That's where the master and mistress exercise their horses.'

The trotting lane was a narrow strip of land about five hundred yards long, enclosed by high stone walls. Alys led Silky through its wooden gate, then put her hands on the pony's back and vaulted lightly into the saddle.

'Come on, Silky, canter,' she whispered; immediately Silky lengthened her stride, and they flew up and down the lane. Alys's linen cap came off, and Francis ran to pick it up. Alys didn't stop for it, though; she knew she looked better with her black ringlets streaming in the wind. There's going to be a gale tonight, she thought, but she didn't care. She loved high winds, and this wind was just adding to her excitement.

'Hang on,' shouted Francis. 'I'll get Sultan, and we can have a race.'

In a few minutes he was back, mounted on a beautiful black gelding. This was even better. Knee to knee they rode, up and down, the wind whipping Alys's black ringlets and Francis's golden curls.

'Bravo!' came a shout from the gate. Alys realised that Conor O'Brien, Sir Charles and Colonel Roberts were standing by the gate, watching them. Instantly she slowed down, feeling rather embarrassed. Máire Rua had said that she could have an hour to herself, but perhaps she shouldn't have ridden there without permission. . . . She jumped down from the pony and walked slowly towards them, leading Silky by the halter.

'You're a wonderful rider, my dear,' said Sir Charles. 'You're like your grandmother. I remember my mother talking about her mother's ponies. She used to tell us stories about Golden Dawn and Golden Noon.'

'Unusual to see a nursemaid riding,' drawled Colonel Roberts, looking down his long nose. Alys decided she didn't like him much. 'Is that your son's pony she's riding, Sheriff?' he added, to Conor O'Brien.

'It's my own pony,' said Alys quickly. I definitely don't like him, she thought.

'This is our cousin, Alys McMahon,' said Francis. 'Alys, this is Colonel Roberts.'

Alys curtsied but said nothing. Colonel Roberts gave her a quick glance and turned his back on her.

'We all ride here,' said Conor O'Brien genially. 'Our roads are bad for carts and chaises.'

'And what a wonderful rider your wife is,' said Colonel Roberts, in oily tones. 'I saw her ride yesterday, and I so admired her.'

He's trying to grease himself into favour with Conor O'Brien, thought Alys. I wonder if he's the man I over-heard plotting murder. . . . There was something metallic about his voice that seemed familiar. But if it had been Colonel Roberts, who had he been talking to? It couldn't have been Sir Charles or Francis – firmly Alys put that thought from her head. She didn't want to suspect either of them. Anyway, it's not my business, she decided. Conor O'Brien is a soldier. He knows who to trust.

'I'll go in now, sir,' she said to Conor. 'It will soon be time to dress the children for the party.'

'See you later on,' called Francis gaily.

* * *

'We're awake,' said Honora, as Alys cautiously pushed the door open. 'Dress me first. I have to wear my blue velvet dress, with the white lace collar.'

Alys dressed the little girl carefully. How Eliza would love a dress like this, she thought. She wondered how much it would cost.

'Let me brush your hair now,' she said aloud. 'We'll just leave a few curls on your forehead, for a fringe, and we'll brush the other curls back.'

'I've got a blue velvet band with pearls on it to keep my hair off my face,' said Honora. 'Put that on me, please, and hand me my gold and diamond ring.'

Alys handed over the diamond ring, which was Honora's prize possession. 'You're ready now,' she said. 'Sit there quietly while I dress Mary and Slaney.'

'Oh, good girl, Alys,' said Máire Rua, coming in, 'you've started to get them ready. Donogh is already downstairs, so I'll help you with Teige and Torlach — those two would try the patience of a saint. Oh, by the way, I've been hearing all about your wonderful riding. Sir Charles and his stepson have been raving about you.'

Alys blushed. 'How old is he, madam?' she said hastily, to hide her embarrassment.

'Who? Francis?' Máire Rua gave a knowing smile.

'No, I meant Sir Charles.' Alys was even more embarrassed now, but she tried to explain. 'It's just . . . he's my cousin, but he seems a lot older than I am. . . .'

'Well, your Aunt Cecilia was much older than your father, and she was married when she was about your age,' said Máire Rua. 'Come to that, I was married at fourteen myself; I've three big sons from my first marriage, you know. Anyway, I suppose Sir Charles was born about 1605 – he must be about forty-five now. And Francis,' she added with a grin, 'is seventeen years old. I asked particularly for your sake. He's just about the right age for you.'

Alys felt embarrassed again, but she laughed. She did like Máire Rua – as her grandmother said, Máire Rua was a character. She liked Conor as well. They were both very friendly, comfortable people, she decided.

She finished dressing fat little Mary, gave her a kiss and stood up.

'Now for those boys,' she said. 'I'm going to promise that if they behave themselves I'll teach them to jump. Let's see if that works. I'll go in myself, but if I can't manage them, I'll call you.'

'That's the spirit,' said Máire Rua approvingly.

There was no sign of Teige and Torlach when Alys went into their room. The first thing she noticed was the cold; the second was that the curtains were blowing. She rushed to the window, dragged open the curtains and found the window wide open. A bar was missing from one side of it, leaving a space wide enough for a small boy to climb through.

Alys stuck her head out. At first she saw nothing, but then she spotted a rope hanging down from the roof, only a foot or two from the window. It was attached to one of the battlements on the old tower, hanging just inside the corner where the new mansion was attached to the tower. It was hard to see unless you looked very closely.

Alys leaned out as far as she could and looked up. Then she saw them. Both of the boys were up on the roof of the old tower.

'Come down at once,' she hissed. 'Immediately, or I'll get your mother.'

For a moment she regretted her words. What if they slipped on the way down? But she need not have worried. They were as agile as a pair of squirrels: they slid down the rope, one after the other, and were in the room before she could change her mind. Teige quickly picked up the bar from the floor and fitted it neatly back into the holes, stuffing the bottom hole with a piece of timber to hold the bar in place.

'We saw you,' said Torlach. 'You're great at riding. Teige and I were watching you. You're better than Francis, even.'

'We're good at riding, too,' said Teige proudly. 'But we don't know how to jump properly,' he added sadly.

'If you get washed and dressed in five minutes, I'll teach you to jump tomorrow,' said Alys severely. 'If you don't, then I'll tell your mother and father that you've been up on the tower roof.'

As meek as angels, they washed their faces and put on their knee-length breeches, their white silk hose, their fine cambric shirts, and their burgundy-coloured velvet doublets. Alys was just tying the coloured ribbons below Torlach's knees, and Teige was putting on his fancy shoes with the rosettes on the toes, when Máire

Rua came into the room. Alys gave a hasty glance at the window, but there was no sign of the rope. She smiled modestly at Máire Rua's praise.

The Hallowe'en party was the best Alys had ever known. Up in the musicians' gallery – a small raised space at the end of the great hall – a man with a fiddle, and his two sons with wooden pipes, played softly all evening; the haunting tunes stayed with Alys for the rest of her life. The table was spread with enough food to feed the countryside for a month. There were roast haunches of beef, roast swans, pies of succulent pork, and apple cakes; there were flagons of wine and ale, and goblets full of blackberry juice for the children.

The hall was crowded with children. Cousins had come from Smithstown, from Duagh and from Inchiquin. Even the three Neylon boys – Máire Rua's children from her first marriage – were there; they were being fostered by the Carrigy family, near Corofin, but they visited their mother often. William, the eldest, was fifteen and quite handsome, but Alys only had eyes for Francis. He was like the sun, she thought: everywhere he went there was joy and laughter.

When the time came for the meal, Alys seated herself with the five younger children – Donogh, of course, insisted on sitting by his father. In a moment, Francis had joined them and was joking with Honora about her diamond ring.

'What a beautiful ring, my lady,' he said, kissing her small fat hand. 'Would you marry me?'

'You'll have to dance with me tonight, and sit beside me, if you're going to be my husband,' Honora said pertly.

'You change places with me, then, Teige, and I'll sit between Alys and Honora,' answered Francis.

Alys was so happy that she almost forgot to eat. She told Francis all about Drumshee, about the ponies, about her family.

'Drumshee must be beautiful,' said Francis. 'I love the countryside. When my father was alive we lived in the country, in Kent, but since my mother married Sir Charles we've lived in London most of the time.'

After the meal came the games. Even Donogh forgot that he was a young man with a sword and raced around, squealing, just like the others. Teige tried to push Francis into the tub of water where the apples floated, and then Francis held him over the tub by his ankles until he yelled for mercy. William Neylon lifted up fat little Mary so that she could sink her new teeth into one of the apples hanging from the wooden beam, and Honora danced energetically with a small cousin from Inchiquin Castle.

'So we're dancing now!' said Francis. 'Well, Honora, if you're not going to dance with me, I'll dance with Alys instead.'

Without giving her a chance to say anything, he caught Alys by the waist and whirled her around the room. The musicians were playing an Irish reel, and Francis seemed to be dancing an English dance, but it didn't matter. Alys had never laughed so much in her life. Up and down the room they went, trying not to bump into any of the other couples. All of the children were dancing, and soon the adults joined in. Máire Rua and Conor were dancing together; Alys saw her deliberately steer him in the direction of a hanging apple, so that he bumped his head, and then he tried to make her duck for a floating apple in the tub. Francis held a dangling apple firmly between his strong white teeth and tried to put it into Alys's mouth; he was trying to say something, but his words were ridiculously muffled, and they laughed so much that they both dropped the apple. Máire Rua saw them, but she just laughed, and Conor poked Francis in the ribs as he jigged past.

The music grew louder and the fun grew more furious. The room became increasingly crowded as guests and tenants arrived. The other servants stood in the doorway until Máire Rua signalled to them to join in. It seemed as if all the world were dancing there in the luxuriant, brightly lit room.

Or almost all the world. As Alys paused beside one of the mullioned windows, to cool her hot face against the cold glass, she caught a glimpse of a figure standing at the gatehouse, talking to a slim young man on horseback.

At that moment a torch outside the gatehouse flared, and she saw that the man on foot was Colonel Roberts. And he was warily looking all around. Quickly Alys shrank back behind the curtains.

The Colonel's glance travelled up and down the castle, scanning every window; then he turned away, apparently satisfied that no one was looking. He took a package from inside the breast of his white shirt and handed it to the horseman.

Chapter Five

Although Alys didn't go to bed until two o'clock in the morning, she was awake quite early. She lay in bed watching the sky lighten to a pale primrose, streaked with fuzzy lines of pewter-coloured cloud. Seen through the tracery of the slender black branches of the leafless ash tree across the road, the sky looked like a stained-glass window, she thought.

Her mind was full of pictures of the night before – of colour and sound – of Francis and her whirling around and around, to the music of the fiddle and the pipes – of laughter and fun, and of the way he had kissed her swiftly on the cheek before she had finally gone up the stairs to bed. And then, like an ominous black shadow over everything, there was the memory of Colonel Roberts at the gatehouse, wary as a thief, handing over a package to the young man on horseback. Alys clenched her hands in an agony of indecision. What should she do? Should she talk to someone?

'I'm not going to think about it,' she said aloud, swinging her legs over the side of the bed. The sky was turning pink. She tiptoed over to the window, the bare floorboards cold under her feet, and looked down.

The grass was grey with frost – not a heavy frost: here and there a jewel of water flickered where the sun had already begun to melt the ice. Alys made up her mind. She would go for a ride before the children were up. They would surely sleep in this morning; none of them, not even Mary and Slaney, had been in bed before midnight.

Quickly she pulled on the woollen hose that her grandmother had knitted for her, and put on her old gown. It, too, had been made at Drumshee; the wool came from the sheep that grazed the hillside, and it had been woven on the old loom in the west room of the cottage. She started to put on her shoes, but then she changed her mind, took them in her hand and stole out of the door. The last thing she wanted was for any of the children to wake. I'll go down by the tower, she thought; then I won't have to pass their doors.

The tower had been built about two hundred years before, Máire Rua had told Alys. When she and Conor had built the new mansion, they had put in doors leading through to the old tower. Now the tower held stores, and Conor's men-at-arms were housed there. Alys slipped through the connecting door; inside the tower there was already a bustle of wakening men, so she put on her shoes and went boldly down the stairs.

When she was halfway down the spiral staircase, she paused on the landing to look out of the narrow window. Suddenly a door opened behind her and Colonel Roberts came out. He was talking over his shoulder in a low, confidential way to someone still inside the room, but he hastily shut the door when he saw Alys.

'What are you doing here?' he asked abruptly.

Mind your own business, thought Alys. 'I'm going to the stables,' she said, and didn't wait for his answer. All the way down the stairs, though, she was conscious that he was still watching her. It was only when she reached the bottom of the tower, and started to pull open the heavy, studded door, that she heard the door on the landing re-open and then close again.

As she came out into the stableyard, she glanced back up at the tower. The grim face of the Colonel was looking down at her from a window; behind him, half-hidden by the curtain, was another man. Alys stared up. Could it be Francis? It was definitely someone tall and slim, and there was something familiar about him, but this man's hair seemed darker. . . . At that moment, the curtains were abruptly pulled shut.

Alys shrugged her shoulders. Even if it was Francis, she thought, there's nothing strange about that. After all, Colonel Roberts is probably his commanding officer.

'Off to see your pony?' enquired John, the head stableman. 'She's a beauty – gentle as a dove. She'll be pleased to see you. She's been looking around her; I think she finds it a bit strange here.'

Alys rushed off to the stables. All her worries about Colonel Roberts went out of her head. Quickly she tacked up Silky and vaulted neatly onto her back.

'You've a great seat on a horse,' praised John. 'Take her slowly through the yard; there's a bit of ice about. She'll be all right on the trotting lane, though. Every inch of that was paved with small flat stones when we laid it out; then we put sods of grass on top of the stones, so now the grass roots grow down below the stones. It makes a great place for the horses and the ponies, no matter how bad the weather is.'

Smoke was beginning to rise from all the chimneys when Alys came out of the stable. She walked the pony slowly across the yard; Silky was as sure-footed as a cat, but Alys would never take a chance with her beloved pet. One of the soldiers came out of the barn and opened the gate for her. She recognised him; he was the man she had spoken to the day before, when she was looking for Mary and Slaney. Suddenly another worry came back into her mind.

'How's your friend?' she asked. 'The one who was sick yesterday?'

The man shook his head with a half-frown. 'He's bad,' he said soberly. 'He was groaning all night, and now he's burning with fever and not making any sense.'

'Alys!' came a shout from the tower door. 'Alys, wait for me. I'm going to exercise Sultan.'

Suddenly excitement blazed up in Alys, like a fire burning up all her worries – all her niggling doubts about Colonel Roberts, all her fears that Mary and Slaney might have caught something from the sick man. What a glorious day! she thought. The sky was pink and blue, the sun was starting to blaze strongly, the grass sparkled like precious jewels and she was going to ride with Francis.

Francis was back in a flash; Sultan was snorting and pawing the ground, already excited at the thought of exercise. John was right – the surface of the trotting lane was perfect. The short grass was almost dry already; the rain of the previous days had flowed away between the small flat stones under the turf. Up and down they sped, trying to outrace each other, their mounts enjoying the fun as much as they did.

'Whoa!' shouted Francis, after about twenty minutes. 'That's enough for now. Look how hot the horses are getting.'

There was steam rising from Sultan's black sides and from Silky's pale-gold hide. Alys slowed down and dismounted, using the mounting block next to the gate.

'I'd better go in anyway,' she said guiltily. 'The children may be awake. I must rub down Silky first, and feed her.'

'I'll come with you,' said Francis. John came forward to take his horse, but Francis motioned him away and went on chatting to Alys while they rubbed their horses down with leather cloths.

'She's beautifully bred,' he said, looking at Silky with admiration. 'How old is she?'

'She's two years old,' said Alys. 'We were going to sell her, but my father and mother have given her to me as a present. I'm paying threepence a week for her,' she added grandly.

'That's a bargain,' laughed Francis, giving Silky a friendly pat.

It's amazing, thought Alys. A couple of days ago I didn't even know him, and now I feel as if he's my best friend. She wondered if she could trust him, if she could share her worries with him.

'You look worried,' said Francis, as if he could see into her mind. 'You've got a frown here, just between your eyebrows.'

With his finger he touched Alys's forehead. The spot felt cold and strangely smooth, even after he had taken his finger away.

She decided to trust him. 'Francis,' she said, 'I'm a bit worried about Teige and Torlach.' The easy one first, she thought. 'I found them on the roof of the tower. They've taken a bar out of their window, and they have a rope hanging from the iron bar that supports the guttering. I don't want to tell their mother, but I don't trust them not to do it again, no matter what I say to them.'

'I'll go up on the tower roof and take the rope away after breakfast,' said Francis. 'I'll put it in your room, under your bed. Yours is the room next to the girls' room, isn't it? I'll have a word with those two boys, as well, and try to frighten the life out of them. Is that the only thing that's worrying you?'

'Francis, do you know Colonel Roberts well? Do you . . . do you trust him?' Alys faltered, looking keenly at him. Was it her imagination, or did his face change? Certainly he looked away.

She followed the direction of his eyes, and saw his stepfather enter the stables.

'Were you looking for me, sir?' asked Francis. Was there a note of relief in his voice?

'I'm looking for Alys, actually,' said Sir Charles. 'I just wanted to remind you, Alys, that I will accompany you to Drumshee today. We will be out on manoeuvres while daylight lasts, but we should be back by four o'clock. Mistress O'Brien says that you can go then. She has gone to visit her relations at Smithstown, but she says to tell you that Bridie will take care of the children after you go.'

'So you and I will ride together again today,' said Francis to Alys, in a low voice, before he followed his stepfather out of the yard. Quickly he kissed her on the cheek; then he was gone.

The day seemed long and a bit dull after that. The children were all tired and inclined to quarrel with each other. Shortly before Alys was due to go home, she found Mary and Slaney asleep, curled up together like two kittens.

'They haven't seemed well all day,' she said to Bridie, with a worried frown.

'Just tired,' said Bridie reassuringly. 'Too much to eat, too late to bed. After all, Mary's only four and Slaney's only three. I'll put them to bed for you.'

'Alys, Francis sent me to tell you that he's ready,' said Donogh, bustling in. 'Hurry up, girl, don't keep us waiting.'

'What do you mean, "us"?' asked Alys, irritated by his pompous manner. She gave a hasty kiss to each of the little girls and ran ahead of him out of the big studded door.

'I'm going with you,' said Donogh importantly, slamming the door behind him. 'I might as well see where you live. It'll be something to do, anyway. Teige and Torlach are just playing stupid games.'

Alys stopped. She had been looking forward to the ride with Francis, and now this bumptious Donogh wanted to come. He would make sure that he was the centre of attention all the time, and she would have no chance to talk to Francis. He might even spoil her grandmother's pleasure in Sir Charles's visit.

'No,' she said abruptly. 'Your mother said nothing about you coming. You stay with the other children. Bridie is looking after you.'

'I'm going,' insisted Donogh, marching towards the stableyard in a determined way.

Alys's heart sank when she saw Michael holding Donogh's small pony, saddled and ready. Sir Charles and Francis were already mounted, and Silky whinnied with excitement when she saw Alys coming. Alys patted her quickly and turned to the stableman.

'Who said that Donogh was going, Michael?' she asked.

Michael looked taken aback. He was very nice, but he was slow, almost simple-minded, and never seemed sure about anything. 'He told me himself,' he said uneasily. 'He told me to saddle his pony.'

Chapter Six

race hadn't really liked Sir Charles. Alys puzzled over it all through the next few days. Grace was always talking about her eldest daughter Cecilia, always yearning for news of her and her family; but now, on meeting Cecilia's eldest son, Grace had seemed stiff and almost unwelcoming. It was partly Sir Charles's fault, of course, thought Alys. He had presented his gifts and messages, but in an absent-minded way, like a man with something else on his mind, and he had not been very affectionate towards his grandmother.

On the other hand, Alys consoled herself, everyone had liked Francis. He had paid her grandmother compliments, and teased her with Cecilia's stories of how Grace had danced all night at Queen Elizabeth's court. He had shown Dermot how to do tricks with a piece of string; he had found a velvet ribbon in his pocket for

Eliza; and he had won Betty's heart by admiring baby Owen.

'That Francis should be an Irishman,' Alys's father had said, after Sir Charles and Francis had gone back to Lemeanah. It was high praise from him, and everyone else had nodded in agreement.

That night, Alys couldn't wait to get up to the loft bedroom that she shared with Eliza. Eliza was asleep, and Alys wanted to think in peace and quiet. She sat down on the wax-sealed sandalwood chest that held all the finery her grandmother had worn when she was Alys's age. Dreamily she began to brush her hair. She thought about Francis — about how his dark-gold hair curled softly around his shoulders, how brown his eyes were, how full of fun he was, how nice it had felt when he had kissed her cheek in the darkness of the farmyard before he rode away. Then he had whispered something to her — and that was what she wanted to think about particularly.

'Could you ever marry an Englishman?' he had said. Every time the words came back to her, a warm glow rushed through her whole body.

But when she went to sleep, it was of Colonel Roberts and of Sir Charles that she dreamt; her dreams were uneasy, and slipped into a nightmare before she woke.

'Dark days,' said Grace, as Alys came into the kitchen the next morning. It was a dark day; the sky was roofed with heavy, soft, grey clouds, and the mist covered everything. 'Best take a covered lantern with you. You might need it on the way home.'

'Just as well we stabled the ponies,' said Niall, when Alys met him in the farmyard. 'It was a bad night. Did you hear the wind? I think we're in for a spell of dirty weather. It's as dark as night today.'

Alys didn't care. In another half-hour she might see Francis again. She sang to herself softly as she tacked up Silky.

'Come on, Silky darling, you might have another ride with Sultan,' she whispered as they crossed the yard together, Silky neatly avoiding the ducks who were dabbling in the puddles.

However, when they arrived at Lemeanah, the stables were empty and there was an unusual quietness around the tower and the barns.

'They've all gone off to do some training,' said John. 'The whole lot of them, the Englishmen as well as our own men. Won't be back for a few days, I heard.'

'What about the sick man?' asked Alys. 'Did he go too?'

John shrugged. 'They took him with them in the cart. I think he's pretty bad. I don't know that he'll last the journey.'

Alys was sorry to hear that, but she was relieved that the man had gone. As long as he hadn't given any infection to the two little girls, she wouldn't worry about him any more.

She had turned to go into the kitchen when John came after her and spoke softly in her ear.

'Don't say anything indoors,' he said; 'least said, soonest mended – but I think that poor fellow had the plague.'

The plague, thought Alys. And Mary and Slaney were bending over him! What can I do? What would Máire Rua do if she knew? How can I tell her without betraying Bridie? What good would it do to tell her now? Maybe John is right: least said, soonest mended. . . .

'Alys!' came a shriek from the kitchen window, and then Honora and Mary and Slaney came flying out, tugging Alys's hands and drawing her into the warm kitchen. To her immense relief, all the children looked very well this morning. Mary and Slaney must just have been tired yesterday, after all, she thought. She bent down and hugged and kissed them. They were so sweet; it would be dreadful if anything happened to them.

'Alys, can we do some riding today?' shouted Torlach. 'Mother says we may if the rain doesn't get worse.'

'I want to jump,' said Teige. 'Will you teach me today, Alys?'

They're very sweet too, thought Alys, tousling their hair and pretending to kiss them as well.

'We're too old to be kissed,' Teige shouted, but they seized her hands and jumped up and down beside her.

'Give me a kiss, too,' demanded Honora.

'Well, aren't you the popular one,' laughed Máire Rua. 'No Francis today, I'm afraid, Alys. Donogh will have to be your young man now.'

'Donogh doesn't like Alys,' said Teige triumphantly.

'Don't be silly. Of course he does,' said Máire Rua. 'Oh, Bridie, are you down there in the pantry? I just want to have a word about Sunday. . . .'

'He said rude words about you,' continued Teige, once his mother had swept out of the kitchen.

'He was being very silly, then,' said Alys, with a glance at the sullen-faced Donogh.

'Well, I'm not the only one who calls you names,' retorted Donogh, sticking out his tongue. 'Colonel Roberts thinks you have long ears. I heard him say that to Sir Charles. He said, "That nursemaid has long ears. I caught her listening outside the door." So there! You don't like that, do you?'

He stared at her triumphantly. He was clever enough to have noticed that she looked taken aback. Why should Colonel Roberts worry about me? thought Alys. Why should he worry about a nursemaid passing his room, unless he has a secret to hide?

'Don't tell tales,' she said crushingly to Donogh. He stuck out his tongue again and waggled his ears at her.

'Mother,' he called, 'will you come for a ride with me? I don't want to go with Teige and Torlach. Alys spends all her time teaching them, or else talking to Francis. She has no time for me.'

'Now, Donogh, I'm sure that's not true,' said Máire Rua, returning to the kitchen. 'Oh, well, come on, then; you come with me. I'm going to see Sarah Queally, and you can be my escort. You must make friends with Alys, though. You can't be with your old mother all the time.'

Again and again, during the next few days, Alys wished that she had tried to make friends with Donogh from the beginning. He was only nine years old, but he had a very high opinion of himself. Máire Rua treated him quite differently from the other children, Alys noticed – almost like an adult; he was her eldest son, and he had to have everything that he wanted. It had been a shock to him when Alys treated him like one of the other children, and he revenged himself by playing spiteful tricks on her – pouring cold water into her soup, jostling her so that she stepped into a puddle and got her feet wet, pulling her hair and then denying that he had done it. Alys didn't know what to do with him.

'You see, if I complain to Máire Rua,' Alys explained to her grandmother on Monday morning, before she left for Lemeanah, 'it won't do any real good. In the first place, she won't believe me; he's always clever enough to make sure that no one sees him do these things, and he'll deny it if she asks him. And, even if she did believe me, she wouldn't like me for it. She adores him; she won't hear a word said against him. Maybe it's because he nearly died of the plague and she saved him. According to Bridie, she nursed him all day and night for a whole week. She never left him for a minute and never slept until he got better.'

'I'd try to make friends with him,' said Grace. 'Could you teach him a clever riding trick — something you haven't taught the other boys? You could say that he's getting a special lesson because he's the oldest.'

'I'll try that,' said Alys, cheering up. 'I think he might be missing the soldiers, too. He loved talking to them. They'll be back on Friday, so I'll see if I can make friends with him by then. He won't want to bother with me once the soldiers are there — he just wants to be a grown-up and be like them. He really is a very grown-up little boy; it's hard to remember that he's only the same age as Eliza.'

'Is he bigger than me?' asked Eliza. She loved to hear stories about the O'Brien children and all the tricks they got up to and all the clothes and toys they owned.

'No, he's not,' said Alys. 'He's the same size as you, or a bit smaller. In fact, Teige's a year younger, but he's quite a bit taller than Donogh, and Torlach, who's only seven, is as big as him. That's another reason, I suppose, why Donogh's so determined that everyone should know that he's the eldest and treat him differently from the other children.'

She was still thinking about Donogh as she tacked up her pony. 'I know what I'll do, Silky,' she said. 'I'll teach him that special trick that I taught you: I'll teach him how to get his pony to walk on its hind legs. He has quite a clever little pony – not as clever as you, of course. I'll tell him that trick will be useful to him when he goes into battle, when he's in his father's regiment. That's all he thinks about these days: being a soldier and marching off to battle.'

The rain fell heavily as Alys rode across from Drumshee to Lemeanah. Several of the fields were flooded, and Alys had to pick her way carefully through the others so that Silky wouldn't sink up to her fetlocks in the soft mud. The sky was black with the promise of more rain to come, and the day was dark, as if dawn hadn't properly arrived. The cows in the fields stood miserably with their heads bowed and their backs to the wind and the rain.

When Alys arrived at Lemeanah, none of the children were looking out of the kitchen window as they usually did. Slightly puzzled, she led Silky into the stable and rubbed her down. One of the stablemen had harnessed one of the big farm-horses to a covered cart and was filling the cart with clean straw. What's that for? wondered Alys. The little covered cart was usually used for the children, but surely Máire Rua wasn't taking the children visiting in this bad weather. There had been no mention of it yesterday.

She ran across the stableyard and went into the kitchen. It was empty – except for Bridie, who was sitting on a chair with her head on the table, sobbing noisily. She lifted her head when Alys came in, and Alys was shocked by her face. She looked as if she had been crying for hours.

'Oh, Alys,' she sobbed. 'The two little ones, Mary and Slaney, are awful bad with a fever. . . . ' She sobbed again and then managed to choke out, 'Mistress is afraid that it might be the plague.'

Chapter Seven

Máire Rua swept into the room, with an air of icy calm about her.

'There you are, Alys,' she said briefly. 'Bridie will have told you we have sickness in the house: Mary and Slaney are ill. I'm sending the other children to my sister at Ennistymon. You must take them there, but you needn't stay; my sister has plenty of servants to care for them. If you prefer, you can go back to Drumshee and stay there until we see what this sickness is.'

'I've had the plague, madam,' faltered Alys. 'I could help you to nurse Mary and Slaney. They're used to me. They'll be happy with me when you need to rest.'

'The plague?' snapped Máire Rua. 'Who said anything about the plague?' Her angry gaze went to Bridie, who sobbed again.

There was a moment's silence. Then Máire Rua shrugged her shoulders.

'It probably is the plague,' she said briefly. 'I hear there was a case of it among the soldiers. Come with me, Alys. We must make sure that the children have everything they need.'

Alys followed her meekly, without daring to glance at Bridie. Donogh, Teige, Torlach and Honora were all in their mother's room, huddled around the fire, too shocked even to cry. At the sight of their faces, Alys went down on her knees and held out her arms. Not just Honora, but Teige and Torlach as well, cuddled against her; only Donogh remained aloof.

'You look after them, Alys,' said Máire Rua, going hastily to the door. 'I'll get Macha to pack their things; she'll know what they'll need. She'll let you know when the cart is loaded, and then you can all be off. I'm going back to Mary and Slaney. Goodbye, children. Behave well for your aunt.'

It seemed to Alys that Máire Rua could hardly bear the sight of the children; the contrast between their health and the feverish faces of the two youngest must be too painful for her. She thought the children understood this too. They all looked frightened, but none of them attempted to kiss their mother or go to her for comfort.

'I'm not going,' said Donogh suddenly.

'Yes, you are,' said Máire Rua, turning back.

'I'm not going,' he repeated, glaring at her.

I suppose he wants to be here when his father and the soldiers come back, thought Alys. He's always thinking of himself.

'I'm not going, Mother!' he shouted, as Máire Rua lifted the latch of the door. 'I'm the man of the house when Father's away. Anyway, I've had the plague. There's no need to send me away.'

At the word 'plague', Teige started to sob. He's old enough to know what it means, thought Alys.

'Have it your own way,' said Máire Rua, as if she could bear no more. 'Stay if you want to stay.'

Abruptly she swept out of the room. Donogh followed her.

'Don't worry, Teige,' said Alys. 'I had the plague, Donogh had the plague, and we're both fine. Now let's think about what you're going to do at Ennistymon. There's a big river, with cascades of water falling down the rocks, just next to your aunt's castle. I hear that salmon come leaping down the cascades. Maybe you could catch one of them.'

'We'll climb out of our bedroom at night and catch one by moonlight,' said Torlach eagerly. 'Jimmy the Bridge says that's the best time to catch a salmon.'

'None of that,' said Alys sternly, remembering the rope under her bed and the dangerous climb to the roof of the tower. 'If you want to go out by moonlight, just ask your aunt. I'm sure she'll allow you if you ask her nicely. She'll get one of her servants who is good at fishing to go with you, and then you'll have a better chance.'

All the way to Ennistymon, Alys talked non-stop, promising the boys all sorts of exciting adventures and assuring Honora that there would be many parties where she would be able to wear her diamond ring and her best silk dress. By the time they arrived at Ennistymon, they were all looking better. Their aunt seemed to be a kind, motherly woman; Alys left them there with an easy mind and set off back to Lemeanah.

She wished she had Silky to ride; the cart jolted along so slowly, and now she had nothing to distract her from the thought of the two lovely little girls who had caught the plague from the soldier in the barn. She huddled down under the covering, glad of the protection against the rain but depressed by the darkness and gloom of the day.

As soon as she arrived back at the castle, she went straight up to the little girls' bedroom on the third floor. She opened the door – and stopped. The room was empty, and the beds had been stripped of their coverings.

Oh, no! thought Alys. What's happened?

'They're in Mother's bedroom,' said Donogh from behind her. He had come silently out of his own room on the opposite side of the passage. His face looked as if he had been crying, and suddenly Alys felt a rush of affection towards him. After all, he was only a little boy, the same age as her own sister; it was silly of her to dislike him as if he were a grown-up.

'Don't worry,' she said, holding her hand out to him. 'You and I had the plague, and we got better.' The more often she said that, the more it gave her hope. 'Come down out of the cold now,' she added. 'Go into the kitchen to Bridie.'

'I don't want to go into the kitchen with Bridie,' said Donogh, with a shake in his voice. 'I want to do something. I want to help.'

There's only one person who might be able to help now, thought Alys. And that's my mother.

At that, a thought came to her. 'Would you be able to ride over to Drumshee with me?' she asked. 'I want to get some of my mother's special fever drink. She makes it from herbs. It cured me and Dermot, my brother, when we had the plague. If you come with me, you'll be able to hold the covered lantern if we need it – I'll have to carry the pot.'

'I'll get my pony saddled,' said Donogh. He clattered down the stairs, looking more like himself.

Alys opened the door of Máire Rua's bedroom and peeped in. 'Donogh and I are going over to Drumshee for one of my mother's fever drinks,' she whispered.

The room was almost dark; she could barely see Máire Rua sitting by the big bed. The curtains around the bed were drawn, but from within them Alys could hear the muttering of a child in a high fever. Máire Rua nodded her head slightly, but she didn't take her eyes from the children.

They sound bad, Alys thought as she ran down the stairs. It's not good when the fever strikes so quickly and so strongly – I'm sure I remember Mother saying that. . . .

* * *

'Lord bless and save us all,' said Betty, crossing herself, when Alys burst into the little kitchen at Drumshee with the terrible news.

She wasted no time, however. In a minute she had taken down a large jar from the dresser, poured some of the fever drink into a smaller flagon and stoppered its mouth with a twist of cloth.

'This will do you for a couple of days,' she told Alys. 'Please God, they'll have improved by then. You can send the lad over for some more if you need it. You'll know the way now, won't you?' she added, to Donogh.

He nodded, but said nothing. He's a very silent child, thought Alys. If that were Teige or Torlach, they'd be looking at everything and bursting with questions.

'Give them a drink of this three or four times a day,' continued Betty. 'Try to get the fever down. Keep sponging them with cool water. If you can get the fever down in five days, they'll get better.'

'And if the fever won't come down?' questioned Alys.

Betty gave a warning glance at Donogh; then, as the latch lifted, she turned to the door.

'Here's our Eliza,' she said with relief. 'She's just your age,' she added, to Donogh. 'I remember your mother riding out, the very day Eliza was born, to drive the English settlers out of their farms and castles – and that was just two weeks after you were born.' She chuckled, and Alys laughed too. Now that she knew Máire Rua, she had often imagined that scene.

Donogh, however, had no interest in Betty's memories. He had nothing to say to Eliza, either. He measured himself against her with one glance, realised that she was taller, and moved away to stand beside the door, anxious to leave. Alys kissed her mother and sister, had a quick peep at baby Owen sleeping peacefully in the cradle, and then followed him out. In silence, they mounted their ponies and rode off down the avenue.

He's a brave boy, she thought as they rode back. The wind was gusting from the northwest and the rain was driving into their faces the whole way back; but, though

Donogh pulled his black cloak tightly around him, he didn't say a word of complaint. His pony had very short legs and made poor progress; time after time, Alys had to hold Silky back so he could keep up.

'You go on,' Donogh said after a while. 'I can see the lights of Lemeanah now; I'll be able to find my own way home. You'll get there a good quarter of an hour earlier if you go on ahead. I'll light the lantern if I need it. I've got my flints and my tinder-box in my pocket.'

'I'd better not,' said Alys hesitantly. Everything in her urged her to hurry; but Donogh was only nine, after all, and the dark day was sliding into night. He might be frightened on his own.

'Do as I tell you,' he said, with his usual lofty air.

Alys shrugged her shoulders. 'Come on, Silky,' she said. 'Canter.'

It seemed as if Silky understood the urgency. In spite of the wind and the rain and the gathering gloom, she shot like a hawk through the fields, over the low hedge and out onto the road. With a thunder of hooves, they were down the road and turning in to the stableyard at Lemeanah.

'Could you look after Silky for me, John?' Alys asked, tossing the reins to the stableman. 'Oh, and send someone out to find Donogh. He's coming across the fields from Drumshee.'

That won't please his lordship, she thought as she pulled off her wet cloak and left it by the fireplace. Still, he is only nine. I don't want him out in the dark and the wind by himself.'

Holding the precious flagon, she ran up the stairs and into the dark bedroom.

'How are they?' she whispered, making her way towards the bed.

Máire Rua said nothing. By the light of the fire Alys could see that her mouth was tightly pursed, her brown eyes were hard and tears were trickling down her weather-beaten cheeks.

'Mother says to give them some of this every few hours, and to try to break the fever,' continued Alys. She could hardly bear to look at Máire Rua's face; she busied herself looking for a spoon on the table by the fireplace. By the time she found one, Máire Rua had wiped her face with a quick, impatient scrub of her sleeve and was propping Mary up to receive the first dose. When Alys put her hand on Mary's cheek, she felt as if the heat would scorch her. Slaney was even hotter, and she seemed as weak and limp as a cloth doll.

Was there any chance that two children who were so sick could recover?

Chapter Eight

The two little girls had fallen ill on Monday. On Tuesday they were even worse, and Wednesday morning brought no change. Alys spent every night in the castle. Her one thought was to help Máire Rua save the two little girls.

'My mother says we have to try to get the fever down in five days,' said Alys, gently sponging Slaney's burning skin with a cool, damp cloth.

Máire Rua said nothing. She had been sponging Mary, but now she dropped the cloth back into the basin and sat with her head in her hands.

'They're worse than Donogh ever was,' she said dully. 'We won't save them.'

Alys didn't know what to do. In spite of the huge log fire that burned in the hearth, the room was not warm; the southwesterly winds rattled at the huge windows and a draught swept in under the ornate door. Mary would get chilled if she was left like that. Quickly Alys finished sponging Slaney, popped her back under the covers and then turned to Mary.

'Leave her,' said Máire Rua, with her head still in her hands. 'You can't cure her. Let her die in peace.'

At that moment, a flash of lightning illuminated the room as brightly as forty candles. It lit up Mary's small body – once so plump, now so thin – and Alys gasped in horror. The light from the window showed her the dreaded signs: Mary had big blue swellings, the size of a pigeon's egg, on her neck.

Gently Alys lifted the child's arms, one by one; in each armpit she found the same lumps. Then she slipped her hand under the covers and felt Slaney's neck. The dreaded buboes were only pea-sized, but they were there. This was definitely bubonic plague. Máire Rua was right. There was little hope of saving the children now.

Forty times during the day Alys checked the little girls, and each time it seemed as if the fatal swellings had got bigger. By evening, Mary's were the size of a chicken's egg and Slaney's were almost as big. It was getting very difficult even to make them swallow the fever drink. Their breathing was fast and shallow, and very loud in that silent house.

'You lie down on the truckle bed for a few hours, madam,' whispered Alys. 'I'll wake you if there's any change. You were awake all last night.'

Máire Rua said nothing, but she lay down on the bed. She did not sleep, though; every time Alys glanced at her, she could see the woman's dark eyes, wide and unseeing, fixed on the ceiling.

About midnight, Máire Rua swung her legs off the bed. 'You go to bed now, Alys. I'll call you at dawn,' she said calmly.

Alys stumbled out and dragged herself up to her room on the third floor. Her legs were shaking, and the candle in her hand wavered, sending huge shadows moving on the walls.

When she reached the top floor, Donogh's door opened and he came out. He was still fully dressed, Alys noticed. He stared at her for a moment, as if he expected her to say something. Alys tried to smile at him, but the muscles of her face felt stiff and frozen. Before she could say anything, Donogh went back into his room and shut the door.

She hesitated for a moment, but then she heard the noise of the bolt being drawn. She went into her own room, threw herself on the bed without undressing and was asleep in a moment.

At first, when she felt a hand shaking her awake, she was bewildered. She thought that she was at home, in Drumshee, and that Dermot had come to call her. The hand was too small and soft to be Dermot's hand, though, and suddenly Alys realised that it was Donogh. She sat up with a start, pushing her ringlets out of her eyes.

'Oh, my love,' she said. 'What's the matter?'

Donogh's eyes were rimmed with red and seemed to have sunk into his face. He bit his lip and made three attempts before he could steady his voice enough to speak.

'Mother has sent for Father Dominic,' he said. 'I couldn't sleep and I went downstairs. John has saddled up and gone off for him. She wouldn't even trust me to do that.'

'John will know best where to find him,' said Alys quickly. 'You know it's a dangerous time for priests; if Cromwell's army come into Clare, they'll be hounded like wolves. You're needed here, anyway. If Mary and Slaney die, you'll be your mother's only comfort.'

'Do you think they'll die?' The words seemed to be jerked out of him.

Alys looked at him. He was only nine, but he was very adult for his age. She owed him the truth.

'I think they might,' she said honestly. 'And then your mother will need you badly. Come down with me now.'

She slipped on her shoes and walked down the stairs, holding Donogh's hand.

Old Father Dominic was already in Máire Rua's bedroom. He must have been close by, for John to find him so quickly, thought Alys. Her eyes went quickly to the big bed with its sumptuous hangings. The children's breathing wasn't as loud as it had been, and for a moment Alys felt a slight spring of hope.

As she moved nearer, though, the sight of the two little girls told her that the end was near. Their small faces were as white as the marble cherubs in Coad Church.

Father Dominic bent over them, muttering Latin words and dipping a piece of bog cotton into the small pot that held the sacred oils. He anointed the children's hands and feet, made the sign of the cross on their foreheads, then knelt by the bedside and began the prayer for the dying.

Loudly and clearly, Máire Rua joined in. Alys tried, but her voice was choked with sobs. She kept her arm around Donogh. He had buried his face in her shoulder, and she pressed her hand to the back of his head.

Suddenly she was conscious that the noisy breathing from the bed had become softer. A moment later, it ceased completely.

'It's over,' said Father Dominic, standing up. 'Two little angels to join God in heaven.'

Alys wished she could whisper some comfort to Donogh, but she was afraid that she would break down if she spoke. She watched through her tears as Máire Rua got to her feet and walked steadily towards the bed.

At that moment, the silence of the bedroom was broken. From the road outside came the rhythm of marching feet and the cheerful note of a trumpet.

'My husband and his troops have come back,' said Máire Rua calmly. 'Will you stay here, Father? I must go and tell him the news.'

With great dignity, she swept from the room. Donogh stood up to follow her, and Alys went with him, keeping her arm around him.

Máire Rua flung open the heavy oak door and stood on the stone step, waiting impassively for the men to file through the gatehouse. Alys watched, holding Donogh against her side. Conor O'Brien, Colonel Roberts and Sir Charles were at the head of the troops, and behind them was a slim young man. But it wasn't Francis – this man had dark hair; it was Cornet Smith, the young man Alys had seen talking to Colonel Roberts on Hallowe'en night. Alys quickly looked down the long line of the regiment, but Francis was definitely not there.

'Here we are, two days earlier than we said,' called Conor O'Brien in his loud, cheerful voice. 'We just came back to get provisions and spare ammunition for our march to Limerick, and to leave three of the men here – they're sick. We can only stay a couple of hours.'

He, Colonel Roberts and Sir Charles dismounted and climbed the steps towards Máire Rua. Her face still betrayed nothing to Alys's eyes, but her husband knew her better.

'Is something wrong?' he asked quickly.

Her mouth tightened, but still she said nothing. She's afraid of breaking down, thought Alys. She herself could not have spoken without sobbing.

It was Donogh who broke the uneasy silence.

'Father,' he said with a sob, breaking from Alys's grasp and throwing himself into Conor's arms, 'my two little sisters are dead.'

Conor's arms tightened around him and he looked at his wife, his face white and wide-eyed. Máire Rua nodded sharply and turned to go indoors. Conor lifted Donogh in his arms and followed her, Colonel Roberts at his heels. Alys moved down the steps. Donogh wouldn't need her now; he would be all right with his father. She could get some fresh air for her aching head.

At the doorway Conor turned and spoke clearly, so that both Sir Charles and Colonel Roberts could hear him.

'I pray you, give us some time alone. I will give orders for everyone to be fed in the tower and in the barns.'

The studded oak door closed gently behind the mourning parents and their son.

Colonel Roberts went back to Sir Charles, and they spoke together in low voices. Then Colonel Roberts went up to Cornet Smith and muttered a few words to him; the young man nodded and went into the gatehouse.

Where is Francis? thought Alys. Is he one of the three sick men?

She waited until Colonel Roberts, followed by Sir Charles, had marched the men around to the tower and the barn. Then she slipped into the kitchen. Bridie, with tears streaming down her face, was busy chopping up cabbage and throwing it into a pot where a large piece of bacon was simmering. Alys went to the table and silently began to help Macha peel and slice potatoes.

While she worked, Alys thought about the sad scene upstairs. They must be in the bedroom, she thought, Donogh with them, reliving the sorrow of the early hours of the morning. Should I make some excuse to go up and take him away? she thought. He can't bear much more sorrow. He's only nine years old.

The thought had hardly crossed her mind when the door was pushed open and Donogh appeared. He was looking a little better, Alys noticed with relief. He probably felt that his father's arrival had taken the burden of responsibility from him. He came straight over to her and stood beside her, leaning against her slightly.

Without hesitation, she put her arm around him. Though he didn't respond, he didn't move away.

'Bridie, my father asks if you could serve a meal for him, Sir Charles and Colonel Roberts in the small parlour,' he said, with some of his old lordly manner. 'They need to get away again in a couple of hours. They want to be at Castleconnell before nightfall.'

'Where's Castleconnell?' asked Alys. She didn't much care, but it would be good to see Donogh taking an interest in the war with the Cromwellians and behaving more like his old self again.

'It's by the Shannon, near Limerick,' he said importantly. 'All the Confederate troops are camped there. Ireton – he's Cromwell's son-in-law – has captured Limerick, and the Confederates are going to lay siege to it. My father has to go; he's leaving me in charge here.'

'Won't he be here for the little girls' burial?' blurted out Macha. Alys kicked her under the table, but it was too late. The brave-young-soldier look faded from Donogh's face and the frightened-child look replaced it.

'He'll be back on Saturday, sometime after noon. He'll stay until Sunday morning for the burial,' he said in a low voice. He slipped away from Alys's arm and went out. Alys heard him sob as he closed the door behind him.

'Stupid,' she said scathingly to Macha. 'Why did you have to remind him and upset him again?'

'Take that tray up to the parlour, Macha,' intervened Bridie, before Macha could reply. 'Alys, you take that small pot of stew out to the barn and send John in for the big pot.'

There was a great buzz of excitement in the barn. All the men seemed to be talking animatedly about the action that lay ahead of them. Alys sent John for the big pot of stew and lingered for a few minutes until he returned.

'Limerick' seemed to be the word on everyone's lips; but then Alys's ear caught some mutterings from two soldiers who had seated themselves behind one of the haystacks. 'Docs Francis Chandler know?' one of them asked. Alys moved closer, but she couldn't understand the other man's reply.

To her disappointment, they said no more about Francis. Alys understood English very well, but the man who was speaking had a strange accent and she could only catch a word here and there. 'Cromwell' – that word was clear; 'Parliamentarians' – that was the name for Cromwell's troops; and then a lot of low muttering in that thick, almost incomprehensible accent. And then silence.

Alys was just about to move away when the other man laughed. 'Old Long-Nose has turned his coat again. It's not the first time. Well, I don't care, as long as I get my wages. Back home in Kent, my brother's for Cromwell.'

'Alys,' shouted John at that moment, and she had to go.

The words themselves had been quite clear; but what did they mean? 'Old Long-Nose' must be Colonel

Roberts, but what was 'turning his coat'? Could it mean that Colonel Roberts had changed sides, from the Confederates to the Cromwellians? If he had, then Conor O'Brien might be in danger from his treachery. . . . I should warn him, thought Alys.

But what if she were wrong? What if she had misunderstood the English words? 'Turned his coat' might mean something quite different. Maybe, she thought, if I can get a moment alone with Conor O'Brien, I can just tell him what I overheard, without making a big fuss about it, and let him decide.

Feeling relieved at her decision, she ran across to John. 'You're wanted in the kitchen,' he told her. 'You're to help Macha serve the meal in the parlour.'

The meal was a silent one. Sir Charles and Colonel Roberts looked ill at ease; Conor O'Brien forced himself to talk to Donogh about pistols; Máire Rua sat tight-lipped and brooding, and ate nothing. It seemed a relief to them all when the noise of marching men outside the window brought them to their feet.

'Stay here,' said Conor O'Brien to his wife. 'Don't come to the door. You stay with your mother, Donogh. Don't forget, you're the man of the house now.'

He kissed his wife and added, in a low voice, 'I'll be back on Saturday afternoon for the wake, and I'll stay for the burial on Sunday. I'll just bring John with me.'

Máire Rua straightened her back. 'Take care,' she said. 'Father Dominic tells me that the Parliamentarians have taken Bunratty and Clonroad in Ennis. You'll run into danger without a regiment at your back.'

'Have no fear for me,' said Conor gently. 'I know this countryside like the back of my hand. I'll come by Killaloe – our troops hold that bank of the Shannon – and then I'll just cut across through Inchicronan Pass. No Parliamentarians will be there; it's too wild and deserted.'

Alys looked at him with interest – she knew Inchicronan, her Aunt Bridget lived there. Then she realised that she wasn't the only one looking at Conor O'Brien. Colonel Roberts was staring at him with a look of speculation in his eyes. Why was Colonel Roberts so interested in Inchicronan Pass?

A minute later, Conor O'Brien, Sir Charles and Colonel Roberts left the room. There were some shouted orders, and the clip–clop of horses' hooves; and then all was quiet again at Lemeanah Castle.

Alys gazed after them. She hadn't found a moment to speak to Conor O'Brien. I'll definitely do it when he comes back on Saturday, she thought.

Chapter Nine

'And with it all, Granny, I never found out where Francis was and what happened to him,' finished Alys. Suddenly she broke down and started to cry. She had told her grandmother all about the death of the two little girls, about the words she had heard on the road after she had first gone to Lemeanah, about everything else she had overheard since – the man who had spoken of the 'victory' at Drogheda, the one who had called Colonel Roberts a turncoat. But now, at the thought that Francis might be lying ill – might be dying of the plague – she could no longer hold back her tears.

'Hush,' said Grace soothingly. 'Hush. Where's my brave girl, now?'

'What will I do, Granny?' sobbed Alys.

Automatically Grace got up and moved the kettle towards the front of the fire. The family would all be home soon, and it would be time for the evening meal.

'Well, the first thing you must do,' she said decisively, 'is tell Máire Rua everything you know. She'll do something about it, if I know her.'

'And what about Francis?' wept Alys. 'I'll die if anything happens to him.'

There was a silence in the little kitchen. Finally Alys dried her eyes and looked at her grandmother. Grace's face looked very tender. She reached over and stroked Alys's hand.

'Francis will be all right,' she said lovingly. 'He may not be one of the three sick men. He may be off on a mission somewhere. Even if he is ill, he's a strong young man. He'll recover. You can ask about him tomorrow.'

'And what if he's a traitor, too? What will I do then?'

'Do you think he is?'

Alys thought. 'No – I don't think so,' she said hesitantly. 'But Sir Charles is his stepfather, and he might have dragged Francis into this.'

'Why don't you ask him?' said Grace calmly. 'Ask him tomorrow, if you see him. And listen to him, mind! Even if he has joined the Cromwellians, that doesn't mean he's plotting to kill Conor O'Brien. It doesn't even mean he's a bad person. In a war like this one, you know, not everyone finds it easy to decide which side is right and which is wrong. Lord Inchiquin, Conor O'Brien's own cousin, has changed sides twice already in these last ten years – first he was for the King, then he was for Cromwell, and now he's for the King again. These are troubled times, and it's hard for even the wisest man to know what's best. And Francis is only seventeen.'

Alys smiled to herself. Her grandmother had a way of making everything seem simple.

'What happens if I fall madly in love with him and I want to marry him?' she asked lightly.

Grace shrugged. 'At your age I knew who I wanted to marry. I think I was in love with Enda all my life, but I decided when I was in England, when I was fourteen. I never changed my mind and I never regretted it. If you're in love with him and want to marry him, then go and do it. It's your life. You're grown up now. You must take responsibility for your own decisions; that's what grown-up people do.'

Alys kissed her grandmother. 'I think I'll go out to see Silky,' she said. 'Then I'd better go to bed. I should be there early tomorrow morning; Máire Rua may need me. There'll be the wake tomorrow night, and then the burial on Sunday. . . . I'll take a little flagon of Mother's fever drink and put it in my saddlebag. If Francis is ill, it will cure him.'

Silky was in the stable, with the other ponies. Alys shone the covered lantern on her pale-gold sides and her muscular legs. Silky's looking wonderful, she thought. The regular exercise suited her; it would have been hard to find a fitter, faster pony.

'Oh, Silky,' she whispered. 'If only you and I and Francis could just gallop away into the sunshine, away from all these problems.'

She rested there for a moment, with her head against Silky's warm side and Silky's soft lips nuzzling the top of her head. Would I still love Francis if he really has changed sides? she wondered.

'I would,' she said aloud.

But then the words she had overheard, all those weeks before, came back to her. 'If Conor O'Brien were to be killed . . .' the unknown voice on that dark evening had said. Could she still love Francis if he were party to that?

Alys had no answer to that question.

* * *

As soon as Alys arrived at Lemeanah in the morning, she stabled Silky, took the flagon of fever drink from her saddlebag and went to look for John.

'John,' she called.

'John's not here, Alys,' said Michael, coming out of the stable. 'He went with the master.'

'Oh, I forgot,' said Alys.

She had to know if Francis was ill. Even though Michael was a bit slow, he might know the names of the soldiers. 'Michael, is Francis Chandler one of the sick men?' she asked boldly.

Michael nodded. 'Yes, he is,' he said. 'He's all right, though,' he added quickly, when he saw Alys's face. 'It's not the plague or anything like that. Just a touch of fever – the Irish ague, all the English soldiers call it. They're not used to so much rain, they say. I was just going to take him some porridge and some hot milk – Bridie has it ready. You bring it up to him; you've a prettier face than I have.'

Alys laughed. She slipped the fever drink into the pocket tied at her waist, and went into the kitchen to get the small pot of porridge and the goblet of hot milk from Bridie.

It was strange to see the tower so empty. Alys's footsteps echoed through the stillness as she climbed the stairs. She was just thinking that she should have asked

Michael which one was Francis's room when a loud sneeze came from behind a door – the door of the room she had seen Colonel Roberts leaving, that morning.

Alys hesitated, and a cold feeling of panic came over her. Sneezing was often the first sign of the plague. . . . Still, it's a sign of the ague as well, she comforted herself. And Michael would know the difference. She knocked boldly on the door.

'Come in,' croaked a voice. It was Francis. He sounded as if he had a bad cold, but at least he was conscious.

'I've brought you some food and something to drink,' Alys said, coming into the room and smiling at him.

The bedcovers were tossed into a wild heap, and Francis's hair and beard were dark with sweat; his lips were dry and cracked, and his eyes looked dull. Alys put the milk and the porridge on the broad windowsill and drew up a small stool beside the bed. Francis wasn't well enough for the porridge, she guessed, but she would give him some of her mother's fever drink, and in a little while he might be able to swallow some milk.

She slipped her hand behind his head – his neck was hot, but not burning, she noticed – and poured some of the liquid between his lips. He swallowed readily. So he can't be too sick, Alys comforted herself.

'Lie still,' she whispered. 'I'll be back.'

Rapidly she ran down the spiral staircase of the old tower and into the kitchen. No one was there, and Alys was thankful for that; she didn't want to answer any questions. Quickly she poured some hot water from the kettle into a leather bucket, took some clean sheets and an old cloth from the huge press by the fireplace and went back to the tower.

When she went into Francis's room, she noticed that he looked a little better; his lips seemed less dry and his eyes were definitely brighter. She sponged his face and neck, and then managed to roll him over so that she could slip the sweat-soaked sheet from beneath him and put the clean one in its place. When she put the milk to his lips, he drank thirstily. Then his head drooped and his eyes shut.

For a moment Alys was alarmed. Was he worse? She touched his neck again; it was definitely cooler. His breathing seemed better as well; it was regular and deep. He was fast asleep.

I'll leave him, then, thought Alys. She was almost glad that she had had no opportunity to ask Francis the questions that she had planned in her mind, over and over again, all through the evening before. I'll find Máire Rua and talk to her about all this, she decided as she went back into the kitchen. Maybe none of the things I've heard mean anything at all, and Máire Rua will laugh at me for being silly; but I don't care. Granny's right: I have to start making decisions and being responsible for them. And when Conor comes back tonight . . .

And then Alys stopped, frozen, in the kitchen doorway. Her heart seemed to stop for a moment and then start beating again, so hard it hurt her chest. An image had flashed into her mind: the look on Colonel Roberts's face when Conor O'Brien had mentioned the lonely pass at Inchicronan. And, all of a sudden, she knew what that look had meant.

I must warn Máire Rua right now, Alys thought in horror; I mustn't waste another minute. 'Bridie,' she said urgently, 'where's Máire Rua?'

Bridie paused in her vigorous scrubbing of the big kitchen table. 'I don't know, Alys. She's gone out, about half an hour ago. I saw her out the window, on that stallion of hers, and Donogh with her on his pony. I said to Macha, "That's a strange . . ."'

But Alys didn't wait to hear the rest of Bridie's grumbling. In a flash, she was back out in the stableyard.

'Michael,' she yelled, 'where did Máire Rua go?'

'I don't know, Alys,' said Michael, coming out of the stable with a leather bucket in his hand. 'She just told me to saddle up the horse and the pony. I didn't dare ask where she was going. She had that look about her, her mouth all pursed up – very fierce, she looked.'

Maybe she's found out about the traitors, thought Alys. Maybe I don't need to do anything; maybe I can just forget I heard anything, just go into the kitchen, help Bridie, look after Francis.

Slowly she walked away. Yes, that's it, she told herself. Máire Rua has found out, and she's gone to warn Conor. It's not my responsibility after all. It's up to her and her husband. There's no one here that I can tell, anyway. Michael's too stupid, Francis is too sick, Bridie can't ride. There's nothing I can do.

Alys stopped by the gatehouse and looked down the road. She stayed there for a few minutes, thinking about the O'Briens. They had become almost as dear to her as her own family.

It was no good arguing with herself. She knew that Máire Rua didn't know about the treachery. If she had, and if she had been riding to warn her husband, nothing on earth would have made her take Donogh into danger.

The most likely thing was that Máire Rua hadn't been able to bear staying in the house with the bodies of her two little dead girls, and had taken Donogh and gone to visit her sister, or her aunt, or her niece. She could be at Inchiquin, or Liscannor, or Smithstown, or Duagh – the O'Briens had relations everywhere. She could be anywhere. And her husband – riding towards the lonely Inchicronan Pass, with only one man at his back – was in deadly danger.

And there was only one person left at Lemeanah who could ride to Inchicronan and warn Conor O'Brien.

Chapter Ten

Twice in the last few weeks, thought Alys as she walked slowly towards the stables, I have been a coward. Each time, I've turned my back and pretended to know nothing. I knew that man had the plague, and I should have told Máire Rua. I knew — I did know, really — that Colonel Roberts, and probably Sir Charles, were planning to murder Conor O'Brien, and I did nothing to warn him. But I still might be able to save him. I know Inchicronan; it's not far from where my Aunt Bridget lives. I'll try to get there and warn him.

As soon as the decision was made, Alys felt better. Gathering up her skirts, she ran to the stables. Silky greeted her with an especially affectionate nuzzle — almost as if she knows I need her now, thought Alys. Quickly she tacked up the pony, jumped on the mounting block and swung herself into the saddle.

The bell of the stableyard clock sounded as she galloped out.

'Eleven o'clock,' said Alys aloud. 'It's a four-hour ride. . . .' There was a terrible fear in her mind. Surely Conor O'Brien would be aiming to be safe home at Lemeanah before darkness fell. He would try to reach Inchicronan before two o'clock.

'Quick, Silky, quick,' she whispered in the pony's ear. 'Canter!'

Silky responded magnificently. Gathering up her haunches, she shot down the road towards Corofin.

It was a dreadful day. A sharp, bitter wind was blowing from the east, directly at them; Alys felt its malice sting her lips and cheeks. She was used to the wind, but usually it was a west wind from the Atlantic, fresh and slightly salty, not like this east wind that seemed to tear her apart. Silky turned her head slightly sideways and lowered her blond eyelashes. Her neat, small ears were flattened against her head.

'I hate an east wind,' Alys remembered her grandmother saying. 'It brings fevers and plagues over from the big cities in England.'

Small flakes of snow had begun to dance on the surface of the wind. Like an army of tiny white tormentors, they swept up against Alys and Silky, getting thicker every moment until they felt like a solid sheet of ice. Alys pulled the hood of her cloak more closely over her face. What would happen if the road filled up with snow? She dared not even allow herself to think about the possibility. If the snow began to lie thickly, she would have to slow Silky to a walk, perhaps even lead her. Snow came very seldom in the west of Ireland; Silky had never seen it before in her life.

She's so brave, though, thought Alys. She must be puzzled; I've never ridden her in weather like this before. Silky's head was half-turned against the stinging pieces of frozen snow, but her flying hooves never slowed or stumbled. On down the road she thundered, past Kilinaboy, past the church at Coad, on to Corofin, over the bridge at the River Fergus.

The turn towards Ruan and Inchicronan should be somewhere around here, thought Alys. She had done this journey often, to visit her Aunt Bridget and her cousins, but she had always been with her family, and usually it had been in summer, with bright sunshine and dry roads. The turn was a small lane, easy to miss in this blinding snow.

Surely I should have come to it by now, she thought, panic filling her mind. In spite of the cold, her hands began to sweat. It seemed ages since she had crossed the bridge, and her memory told her that the turn-off had been almost immediately beyond the river. Then her ear caught the tolling of a bell to her right, not far ahead. Midday already! That must be Rath Church. She had gone much too far. She would have to retrace her way.

Quickly she wheeled the pony around. 'Come on, girl,' she whispered. 'Everything depends on us.'

Silky galloped on, her head low, at a steady pace. Alys could see that her ears were laid flat against the harsh east wind. Alys's fingers were frozen on the wet reins, and she was soaked through, but she never thought of turning back. She had to save Conor O'Brien's life.

She dug her heels in and urged Silky on. 'Come on, girl,' she cried. 'Faster!' She stood in her stirrups, leaning forward on the pony's withers, spreading her weight over the whole of the pony's back. She must do everything she could to make this punishing pace easier for Silky.

By the time they reached Inchicronan Pass, the snow was beginning to lie, filling the hollows in the uneven ground, making it treacherous. Alys slowed Silky to a walk and dismounted.

'That's Inchicronan Pass ahead now, Silky,' she whispered – and then she suddenly reined the pony in. A gleam of silver had caught her eye in the centre of the pass. She held her breath and peered through the dancing shapes of the snowflakes.

She could see the whole of the pass; it was only about a hundred yards long, a narrow stretch bordered by the white shapes of rocks and bushes. Then one of the bush-like humps behind a rock suddenly moved and showed a patch of brown. There are men hiding there, Alys thought, men in brown cloaks; they've been crouched there for some time, so that the snow has fallen on their backs and made them almost invisible.

Instantly Alys made up her mind. We won't go through there, she thought. I know who might be lying hidden behind those rocks.

Taking a firm grip on Silky's bridle, she turned the pony's head towards the north. There was a way around the pass; she had often ridden it with her cousins. Could she find the path now, go around the pass, meet Conor O'Brien, warn him of his danger and lead him back by that same path?

There it is, she thought. I'd know that thorn-bush anywhere; I remember the twisted shape of it. If I go around that bush, I'll find the sheep-path that leads up the hill and down the other side.

Did she dare to ride? The way was steep and rocky, and the ground was treacherous with snow; but if she walked she would be dangerously slow. Conor O'Brien could reach the pass at any moment.

Alys made up her mind. She would trust Silky. There was a strain of Connemara pony in her breeding, and that made her strong and sure-footed. Quickly she vaulted onto the pony's back and urged her on.

The sheep-path was narrow and overgrown with hazel bushes. Several times Alys had to lie almost flat on Silky's back to avoid being whipped across the face by their brittle branches. Silky continued on, going so fast that it was as if she understood the deadly terror in her young mistress's mind.

When they reached the top of the hill, Alys slowed down for a minute to let Silky catch her breath and prepare for the perilous journey down the steep slope. There was no question now of allowing Silky to gallop; this path had to be taken at walking pace. They seemed to go agonisingly slowly.

From time to time, Alys glanced down. She could see the men quite clearly now – she could even see their faces; there were ten or fifteen of them crouching there. If they looked up, there was a chance that they would see her. Silky's blond hide would merge with the snow, but Alys's red cloak would still show through the white flakes.

The men didn't look up, though. Every face was turned towards the east. They were waiting for Conor O'Brien to appear. Alys wished desperately that she could urge Silky into a gallop. She had to get to the other side of the pass before Conor arrived.

And then, as she neared the edge of the pass, a figure in a dark cloak came riding swiftly down the road, towards the narrow gap in the mountains. Alys stared at him in an agony of suspense. Was it Conor? It didn't look like him. The shape was wrong: this was an older man, surely, riding hunched over on a brown horse. Conor was only thirty-three and he always rode a magnificent grey stallion.

Alys hesitated. This might be just some farmer, riding home after checking on his cows or sheep. She glanced at the Cromwellian soldiers lying in wait. No gun was lifted; no orders were whispered. They didn't think it was Conor O'Brien either.

Then she saw the second man – and this time it definitely was Conor O'Brien, on his grey stallion. He rounded the corner and rode straight towards the pass, going quickly. Suddenly Alys knew who the first man was: it was John, of course. His hood was pulled tightly over his head, but she should have recognised the horse.

There was no time to be lost. Conor was very near the pass. Alys stood up in her stirrups and screamed with all the strength of her lungs.

'Go back! Go back!' she yelled. 'They're lying in wait for you. They're hiding behind the rocks. They're over there, in the middle of the pass!'

And then everything happened at once. A gun was lifted – a shot rang out – John fell to the ground. He lay there, very still. Alys felt tears run down her face. Was he dead?

Conor O'Brien spurred on his horse. 'John,' he shouted. 'John!'

'Go back,' sobbed Alys, urging Silky down the last few yards of the path. 'Go back! They'll kill you, too. You're the one they want to kill.' She had little hope that he would listen to her, though; she knew how brave Conor was, and how important his men were to him.

Conor shot past her and galloped towards John. Without slowing his horse's pace, he leaned down from his saddle, grabbed a fistful of John's clothes, hoisted him across the stallion's back and galloped on.

He had no chance, no chance at all. Another shot rang out. Conor's head jerked back; John's body dropped from his grasp like a bag of potatoes; and then Conor slumped in the saddle.

Never had Silky covered the ground so quickly. Alys was beside Conor O'Brien in a second. His eyes were open and he tried to smile at her. Frantically she tried to hold him upright.

'Can you ride?' she said, but she knew it was useless.

The Cromwellian soldiers knew it too. They came out from behind the rocks, their muskets swinging carelessly in their hands.

'He's done for,' said the metallic voice of Colonel Roberts. 'He's been hit in the chest; he'll be dead in a few minutes.'

'This one's dead already,' said Cornet Smith carelessly. With the toe of his boot, he disdainfully turned over John's body. The wide, unseeing eyes glared at the leaden sky.

Alys choked back a sob. 'Lift Colonel O'Brien down from his horse,' she said to a man beside her. He signalled to one of the other men; and then Alys realised that the man she had spoken to was Sir Charles, her own cousin.

'Traitor,' she hissed. She didn't care what she said; she was so overwhelmed at her failure to save Conor O'Brien that she had no fears for herself.

Still holding Silky's bridle, she knelt in the snow next to Conor. Sir Charles turned his back and strode away,

and Colonel Roberts hurried after him. The Cromwellian soldiers drew back a little. They were just waiting for Conor to die; Alys knew that.

An ominous red stain had spread all over the breast of his tunic and soaked the edges of his cloak. His breath came in great sobbing gasps. If there had been any chance that he might recover, the Cromwellians would have fired again.

'Alys,' he whispered, a thin thread of sound. She had to put her ear to his mouth to hear him.

'Yes,' she said. 'I'm listening.'

'Go back to Lemeanah,' Conor said slowly and painfully. His breath was beginning to gurgle in his chest. 'Tell Máire Rua . . . tell . . . all my love . . . best wife . . . a man ever had. . . .' The words came slowly, broken by long pauses while he sucked in breath; but his next words were clear and distinct – an order, not just a dying wish.

'Save Donogh – save my son,' he hissed. 'Go now.'

Alys didn't hesitate. She could do no more for the father, but perhaps she could save the son. She gave a rapid glance around. Colonel Roberts and Sir Charles were talking earnestly, their backs to her; the soldiers had drawn back into the shelter of the hillside, and they also had their backs turned. With one quick movement, Alys was on Silky's back, lying low over the pony's neck and galloping as hard as she could to the west, back towards Lemeanah.

'The girl, sir!' shouted a startled voice. A shot rang out, but it whistled over Alys's head.

'Don't shoot!' yelled Sir Charles. 'That girl is my cousin. Don't shoot, I say!'

Who's in charge? wondered Alys. Surely it's Colonel Roberts. . . . She would hear his metallic voice in a minute, and then a hailstorm of bullets would fly along the narrow pass.

'Come on, Silky,' she whispered. 'You've never let me down yet. My life and Donogh's life depend on you.'

And Silky galloped as no pony ever galloped before.

Chapter Eleven

The journey back was much easier than the journey out had been. The terrible, cutting east wind was at their backs now, its force urging them on. The snow seemed to be lessening and the road towards Ruan was good. Alys and Silky flew down it, Silky's shoes making a continuous drumming sound above the noise of the wind in the trees.

Did Francis know about the treachery? Alys couldn't banish the question from her mind. If he did – if he had been a party to the murder of Conor O'Brien – she couldn't love him any more. But as soon as the decision was taken, she thought of Francis – of his golden hair and his kindness and his merry laugh – and she gave a little moan of pain.

Silky turned her head to look back, and Alys patted her neck. 'Ride on, girl,' she said absent-mindedly. She set her lips in a straight line. I won't think about Francis, she thought. I won't think about John, I won't think about Conor O'Brien; I'll just concentrate on getting to Lemeanah ahead of the Cromwellian troops. I must tell the news to Máire Rua, so that she can save Donogh. Alys stared straight ahead, between Silky's ears, and willed herself to be strong.

Silky turned her head again, as if she heard something behind them. Alys held her breath. Yes: another set of hoofs drummed on the road behind her. Someone was following her, on a large horse, by the sound. Could she ever outdistance him?

She risked a glance over her shoulder. By his dress, it was one of the officers. I know that horse, she thought, and glanced back again. It was Sir Charles's horse, the dappled grey. She had often admired it in the stables.

'Alys,' shouted Sir Charles. 'Alys, wait! I won't hurt you. I promise.'

Alys slowed down. It was no good trying to escape, she knew. Silky could never outdistance that large and powerful grey. Perhaps she could trust Sir Charles; after all, he had saved her from being shot back at Inchicronan Pass. And he seemed to be alone.

'Alys,' he gasped, as he pulled up beside her. 'You must go to your father's sister, your Aunt Bridget. She lives that way. You'll be safe there. I'll get a message to your family. Don't go back to Lemeanah for a few days. Conor O'Brien is dead.'

He thrust his hand into the breast of his doublet, pulled out a purse and handed it to her.

'Give this purse of gold to my stepson, to Francis, if you happen to see him. Tell him that there is no future for the Royalist cause, here or in England. Tell him that he is welcome to join me and Ireton at Limerick; but if that isn't what he wants, he should get a ship from Liscannor, go to France and join his father's brother, who is in Paris with Lord Inchiquin. If you don't see Francis again, give the money to your grandmother.'

With these words, Sir Charles turned his horse around and galloped back towards the pass.

Alys didn't hesitate. She could go to her Aunt Bridget – she had thought of that briefly as she galloped away from the bullets at Inchicronan Pass – but she knew she had to save Donogh, and that meant getting back to Lemeanah before the Cromwellian soldiers arrived. She dug her heels into Silky's sides.

'Come on, girl,' she cried.

The snow began to fall again as Alys cantered through the village of Corofin, and by the time she reached Coad it was coming down in big, thick, soft flakes. The wind had died down, and Silky had at last begun to tire. Alys didn't urge her on; she knew that Silky was going as fast as she possibly could. She herself felt stiff and sore, and she was conscious that every nerve and every muscle in her body was tense with anxiety. Would they be in time?

She strained her ears for the sound of the soldiers. Not all of them had horses, she guessed. But surely the officers would ride ahead if it was important to secure Conor O'Brien's heir. . . .

The sky was beginning to darken by the time Alys reached Lemeanah. She drew in a great sigh of relief when she glimpsed its grey bulk through the dancing flakes of snow. Soon the responsibility would be off her shoulders. Máire Rua would know what to do.

'Máire Rua's not back yet, Alys,' said Michael, as soon as she trotted into the stableyard. 'Bridie's been looking for you everywhere. I told her you might have gone home.'

Alys stared at him, aghast.

'Not back?' she said blankly. 'But she must be. It's almost dark.'

'Go and have a look down the road,' said Michael. 'I'll rub down the pony for you. I've had nothing to do all day. I won't feed her, she's too hot; I'll just let her have a little drink.'

Alys stared at him wordlessly. In the worst moments of her journey back, she had never imagined this. She had rehearsed what she had to say hundreds of times, while they pounded along the road – and now Máire Rua wasn't there to hear it.

The important thing, she thought, is to find Donogh and stop him from coming back to Lemeanah. Maybe I could try to go over to Inchiquin, or send Michael to Duagh and then on to Liscannor. Or I could go up to the tower and find Francis – if he's better, he could give me advice. . . . She took a step towards the tower, and then stopped. She didn't know whether she could trust Francis or not. Whatever was to be done, she had to do it herself.

'Don't unsaddle her, Michael,' she said after a minute. 'I may have to ride her again. Just rub her down and let her walk around. I'll go out to the front and see if there's any sign of them.'

Miserably Alys walked around to the front door and stared down the road towards Coad. Was it her imagination, or was there something in the distance? She strained her eyes.

Too small a dot to be the Cromwellian soldiers, she thought. Hope began to rise in her. Yes – it was Máire Rua, with Donogh beside her! What a tiny child he looked, seated on his small pony!

Hugging her warm red cloak around her, Alys walked down to the gatehouse. She would wait there for them; they wouldn't be long, they were already coming up the path. How was she going to tell Máire Rua that she was a widow and that her children were fatherless? Alys shut her mind firmly on the tender words of love that Conor had spoken. There would be time to tell those afterwards. The first thing was to save Donogh. Máire Rua would know what to do; she would probably send him with Michael over to his aunt at Inchiquin Castle, or to Conor's cousin at Duagh Castle.

And then the worst happened. Around the corner of the Corofin road came a party of horsemen. They weren't riding fast; but, nevertheless, they would be at the door of Lemeanah Castle almost as soon as Máire Rua.

Alys darted out of the gatehouse, ran down to the gate and caught hold of Máire Rua's bridle.

'Madam,' she said in an urgent whisper, 'your husband has been shot. Colonel Roberts and Sir Charles have betrayed him. Now they're coming for Donogh.'

In a flash, Máire Rua had dismounted from her black stallion.

'Give me the pony, son,' she said quickly, lifting Donogh off his pony. Her weather-beaten face held no trace of emotion; only resolution showed in the tight mouth and the bold eyes.

'Go with Alys,' she ordered. 'She and Michael will take you to Inchiquin. Alys, take him to the kitchen; I'll bring them into the parlour, and then you can slip out to the stables. Michael will take Donogh on his horse. Go, son, go quickly.' With that, she leaped onto her horse, wheeled around and galloped back towards the oncoming horsemen, leaving the pony nibbling at the small plants in the wall by the gate.

The soldiers saw her; there was a shouted command, and a party of horsemen galloped forward to meet her. Alys grabbed Donogh's hand and pulled him quickly up the path. The soldiers were already near the gate, and Máire Rua was bellowing at them in a voice like a hunting horn, ordering them off her property. Alys dragged Donogh through the front door, slammed it shut and bolted it after her. This would give them a few more minutes.

She could hear Bridie in the kitchen. 'Lord Almighty,' she was saying to Macha, 'look at all those soldiers running outside the window. Where in the world have they come from? They're not the master's men.'

It's no good going to the kitchen, thought Alys. The soldiers are everywhere. I'll hide him in my bedroom. They won't bother with a servant girl like me. One glance had been enough to show her that neither Sir Charles nor Colonel Roberts had been amongst the party of horsemen. Ashamed to show their faces, she thought grimly as she clattered up the wooden staircase, dragging Donogh behind her.

He hadn't said a word, she realised. Had he heard what she had said to Máire Rua? She looked back and saw silent tears running down his face. She ached with pity for him, but no one had time to comfort him. His life must be saved. Child though he was, he was now the leader of his kin-group. Conor O'Brien's regiment could regroup around his nine-year-old son. The Cromwellians would want to capture him. At best, they might just send him to England, or put him in some dreary prison. At worst, they would kill him.

'Go in there, Donogh,' Alys said urgently, when they reached her room. 'Hide under my bed, and I'll come for you when the soldiers have gone.'

Rapidly she pulled up the cotton bedcover; and then she stopped. Underneath her bed, neatly coiled, lay the rope that Francis had placed there – the rope that Teige and Torlach had been using to climb up to the roof of the tower. Suddenly an idea came to Alys.

She pulled out the rope. It was very long. She remembered the length of it, snaking into the little boys' bedroom; it had been at least twice the length that they had needed to get onto the roof.

'Quick,' she whispered. 'Come on. Don't say a word.'

She opened the door of her bedroom and looked up and down the empty passageway before dragging Donogh out and pulling him rapidly across the corridor, into Teige and Torlach's room. She went to the window and looked down. There was no one in the corner between the tower and the new mansion. The corner was dark, and no snow had clung to these northwestern walls. If the rope reached the ground, she and Donogh might be able to reach the stables without being seen. There was no sign of the Cromwellian soldiers around the stables, either; they must have searched them already.

'It's a long way down,' whispered Donogh. His face looked white in the dim light from the window.

'We can do it,' whispered Alys. 'I'll go first. No one will see us.'

At least Donogh's cloak is black, she thought; it's a pity mine is red. But she was reassured by a quick glance down. The dark day was fading into night, and the dim

light had taken the colour from her cloak; in the shadowy corner, it would just look grey. Quickly she tied the rope to the leg of Torlach's bed, then removed the loose bar from the window and dropped the rope out. She and Donogh both held their breath as the rope fell, uncoiling rapidly. Would it reach the ground?

Not quite – but it came within a few feet of it. There won't be any problem, thought Alys; I'll go first, and I can easily catch Donogh if the last jump is too much for him.

'You know how to go down a rope,' she told him firmly. He must have climbed that rope of Teige and Torlach's, she thought. He can't have been good and well-behaved *all* the time.

Donogh nodded slightly, and Alys felt reassured. 'You won't slip; I'll be below you,' she whispered, as she climbed out of the window and took a last look around. There was no sign of any soldiers.

It's lucky that my hands are so hard from riding, she thought as she inched her way down the rope, hand over hand. The ground was a long way down; hastily she turned her eyes from it and looked up. Donogh was on the windowsill. He had edged his way along it and closed the window behind him as well as he could. I suppose he thinks they might notice if it was open, Alys thought. He's quite bright for his age – and quite brave.

She paused for a moment and gripped one of the pipes that led down from the gutters. She had better keep the rope steady while Donogh began his climb.

'Good boy,' she whispered, as he moved slowly down towards her – he was able to swarm down the rope quite well, she noted with relief. She began moving steadily downwards again, doing her best to stop the rope swinging too much.

The climb seemed to take hours, but Alys knew that the price of rushing could be a broken leg or arm for her, and worse for Donogh. So she crept cautiously down the rope, making sure that each hand had a firm grip before she moved the other.

When she reached the end of the rope, Alys looked down. The drop to the ground was only about six feet, she guessed – nothing to her; but Donogh was so small. . . .

Lightly she jumped, landing with a spring. 'Wait,' she whispered, and dashed into the stables. Michael was still there, she was relieved to see, patiently walking Silky around. He was very slow, Michael, but you could always rely on him to carry out an order once he understood it. He had left Silky saddled and ready to be ridden again.

'Give her to me,' Alys hissed, jumping onto the mounting block. In a second she was on Silky's back and walking her out to the dark corner between the two buildings.

'Let yourself down carefully onto Silky's back, Donogh,' she whispered. Almost instantly, Donogh's feet were in front of her. Silky stood like a statue while the small boy eased himself down. Alys gripped him around the waist, and in a minute he was sitting in front of her.

'I'm going to put my cloak around you,' she said into his ear in a low voice. 'Keep your head hidden under it. We must get past the soldiers.'

Treading delicately and carefully, Silky carried them both around the corner of the new mansion – and then Alys checked her. She had planned to ride out onto the road to Coad and then turn off towards Inchiquin Lake; but the pathway to the gate was full of soldiers, and each one of them held a flaring torch in his hand. They were obviously beginning to search the house and the surrounding land for Donogh. Worse still, a long line of soldiers was marching down the road towards Inchiquin Lake.

There was no chance that Alys would be able to get Donogh past them. And she couldn't take him to Inchiquin Castle. The soldiers would be under orders to search it.

Chapter Twelve

It only took Alys a minute to decide. She went through the vegetable garden and out the little wicket gate, and then turned west. She would take Donogh to Drumshee.

What she hadn't taken into account was his pride and his stubbornness. As soon as they were safely on their way down the road to Kilfenora, his head came out from under her red cloak.

'Where are we going?' he demanded.

'To Drumshee,' said Alys briefly, looking back over her shoulder to make sure that none of the Cromwellian soldiers were following them.

'To Drumshee?' Donogh repeated with disdain. 'What shall I do there? Your people are too poor, too lowly to protect me. I must go to my father's people. I must take charge of his regiment. I must look after my mother and my brothers and sister. I am now the O'Brien of Lemeanah.'

You'll be a dead O'Brien of Lemeanah if you're not careful, thought Alys. She had to bite her lips to stop herself saying it aloud. She was tired to the bone, every nerve in her body seemed tightened to screaming pitch, and she couldn't cope with Donogh and his moods at the moment. She opened her mouth to say something, but then closed it. A quick glance down had shown her that his face was white and streaked with tears.

'I'll take you there as soon as it's safe,' she promised.

'No, I want to go there now,' Donogh insisted, struggling to get free of the arm that she had around him.

Alys made no reply. She stared ahead at the sky, a leaden, lowering sky filled with snow clouds. She desperately wished that she were at home, where her father and mother could share this burden with her. Too much had happened during the last few days. She still didn't know about Francis. Was he alive, or . . . Even in her mind, she couldn't finish the question. And she didn't know whether he had changed sides in this war – or whether, worse still, he had been part of the conspiracy to murder Conor O'Brien.

'Stop it, Donogh,' she said aloud. Donogh continued to struggle and twist within her grasp. Alys gave one last hunted glance over her shoulder – at least there was no sign of pursuit – and then turned in at the gap that led through the fields and across the hill to Drumshee.

Silky stumbled and lost her footing on a hidden rut in the boggy field. Alys's patience finally reached its limit.

'That's your fault!' she snapped. 'You behave yourself or I'll just hand you over to those Cromwellian soldiers.' Lifting her riding whip, she gave Donogh a small tap on the leg. Instantly he stopped struggling. Alys could hear him sobbing quietly. She felt ashamed of herself; he was only a child, after all.

But I have to get him home safely, she thought. My mother will think of something when we get home. She's always so sensible, so full of good ideas. I'm just too tired to think. And he's making everything worse. I'm only five years older than he is; why should I have to look after him? I don't even want to speak to him again. I'm sick of Donogh.

And then the thought of Conor O'Brien's last words – 'Save my son' – came back to her, and a sob escaped her. She had failed to save the father; she must not fail with the son.

'I'm sorry for smacking you, Donogh,' she whispered.

'I'm sorry, too, Alys. I'll sit still now. I didn't mean to hurt Silky,' he said, his voice choked with sobs. Alys bent her head and kissed his forehead.

'Don't worry,' she said. 'We'll soon be at Drumshee. We'll be safe there.'

But will he be safe? she thought. Won't Drumshee be one of the places they'll search for him?

'Will I be?' Donogh asked, echoing her thoughts.

'Yes,' she said firmly. 'My father has a gun.'

He said no more, and Alys concentrated on guiding Silky. Poor Silky, she thought; she must be as tired as I am, but she never loses her temper. The snow on the ground was confusing the pony; she couldn't pick her way with her normal sure-footedness.

'Only another mile to go, girl,' Alys said gently, stroking the pony's blond mane.

When they breasted the top of the next hill, they could see the lights of Drumshee. My father will be in the cowshed with his covered lantern, thought Alys. Granny and Mother will be in the kitchen, cooking bacon and cabbage over the fire; and that's probably Dermot in the stable, with his little lantern. Alys kept her mind firmly on the homely details, picking out familiar landmarks as if she had been away for ten years rather than ten hours. I won't think about Francis until tomorrow, she promised herself.

At the gate, Alys slipped off the pony's back and led her up the hill; the avenue to the cottage was too steep for Silky to carry two. Donogh seemed almost asleep, sitting with his head sunk on his chest and the hood of his cloak covering his face. He roused himself briefly when Dermot came out of the stable, open-mouthed; silently he allowed Alys to lift him down, while Dermot took charge of Silky.

'Everything all right?' asked Betty as they came into the kitchen. Alys signalled to her from behind Donogh's back, and saw her mother's face change. She and Grace exchanged glances.

'Oh, good, supper,' said Alys brightly. 'I'm starving. I'm sure you are too, Donogh.'

Donogh shook his head. 'No,' he said. 'Where's my bedroom? I want to be by myself.'

Betty looked at him in astonishment, and then at Alys.

'Take him upstairs, Alys,' said Grace quietly. 'He can rest up there.'

Now this is a problem, thought Alys. We have no spare room; Dermot sleeps on the settle bed in the kitchen, Granny sleeps in the west room, Mother and Father in the east room, and Eliza and I upstairs. She said nothing, however; she just escorted Donogh up the ladder and showed him her bed.

'Lie down there,' she said briefly. 'Have a rest, and I'll bring you something to eat when you wake up.'

I'm sick of him, she thought again, but I must look after him until I get him to safety.

When she came downstairs again, her father had come in from the cowshed. 'What happened?' he asked.

Suddenly Alys started to cry.

'It's terrible,' she said. 'Conor O'Brien has been shot, and there are Cromwellian troops at Leméanah. Máire Rua asked me to take Donogh to Inchiquin, but I couldn't; the soldiers were blocking the road, and they were going towards Inchiquin. I had to bring him here. He might be killed otherwise. But how are we going to hide him?'

'I wonder if we could make a little place out in the cowshed,' said Niall. 'One of us could keep watch for the soldiers – you'd do that, Dermot, wouldn't you? He wouldn't have to stay there for too long. I could pile up some hay, and he could hide behind it.'

'He'd never do that,' said Alys. 'He has a great opinion of his own dignity. He'd never want to hide in a cowshed.'

'I've an idea,' said Betty slowly. 'We'll see no one tonight, or tomorrow either. They'll try Inchiquin, Duogh, and Liscannor first, before they ever think of coming here. They might never come; but if they hear from some loose-tongued person that you're the children's nurse-maid, they might try looking here eventually. But in the meantime, Niall, you could build some sort of cupboard in Alys's room. The ceiling is very low; it wouldn't take you too long. If the soldiers come, we can shut the boy in there and push the bed in front of it, or something like that. He'll have plenty of air if you take a board out of the ceiling and leave it open to the roof. Anyway, he'll only have to stay there for a little while; it won't take them long to search this place.'

'That's a great idea,' said Niall. 'He'd be warm and comfortable there. I'll tell you what I'll do; I'll build two stone walls attaching the back of Alys's clothes press to the chimney breast, with a few feet of empty space in between. It'll look as if the press is just built into the wall. And I'll loosen one of the boards in the back of the press, so that the boy can get in and out quickly and easily. We can put in that old wooden chest of yours, Mother, so he'll have something to sit on.'

Alys nodded. The chest stood in her room; since she was very small, she had known that it held the beautiful dresses her grandmother had worn at Queen Elizabeth's court. 'When you're getting married,' Grace had always told her, 'we'll open the chest and you can choose your favourite dress for your wedding day.'

The work began that night, before anyone even sat down to supper. Niall, Betty, Alys, Dermot and even Eliza went in and out of the house a hundred times, taking stones from the wall of the small herb garden and bringing them into the kitchen.

'We'll have to get them upstairs tomorrow, and that will be a hard job,' warned Niall. 'Don't take too many big ones.'

Before he sat down to supper, he mixed lime and clay for the mortar, and put some lumps of lime to soak in buckets of water. 'We'll have to limewash the whole room, or even the whole house, as soon as we've built the cupboard,' he said. 'That way, it won't show up as new.'

Donogh refused all food that evening; he just drank water. Eliza and Alys moved into their grandmother's bedroom and left him upstairs. It'll be the safest place for him once the cupboard is built, so he might as well stay there now, thought Alys.

The next morning the work began. Donogh lay on Alys's bed and watched sullenly while Niall rigged up a pulley, using the wheel from the donkey-cart. A rope was passed around the wheel, and a basket was tied to one end of it.

'I'll fill the basket and then haul on the free end of the rope, and you others can unload the stones upstairs,' ordered Niall.

The work had gone on for about half an hour when Alys's patience snapped.

'For goodness' sake, Donogh, get out of bed and help,' she said scornfully. 'I bet if your mother was here, she'd be carrying stones too. Eliza is helping; why can't you? We're doing this for you, remember.'

'I'll spoil my clothes,' said Donogh sulkily.

'I'll lend you my old breeches and shirt,' said Dermot cheerfully. 'Come on, they're in the press in Mother and Father's room.'

The sight of the elegant Donogh swamped in Dermot's outgrown breeches and torn shirt was comic enough to restore Alys's good humour.

'Come on,' she said encouragingly. 'We're starting to build the wall. You and Eliza can put the smaller stones in between the rows of big ones. You'll be a great help.'

'The O'Briens were always a great family to work,' said Grace, from down in the kitchen. 'Many a time I've seen your grandfather, Donogh, out swinging an axe with his men.'

Donogh said nothing, but Alys was amused to notice that he immediately picked up the largest stone he could manage and carried it across to the wall, which was already a couple of feet high.

The work went on steadily all day and all the next morning.

'Time to put the chest in,' said Niall. 'And then I'll attach the press in front of the opening.'

There was a creaking on the ladder, and then Grace's head came up through the hatch. Painfully she hauled herself up into the loft and stood panting for a moment.

'I'm getting old,' she said.

'You're only seventy–seven, that's not old,' teased Niall.

'Alys must have her dress before the chest is put in there,' said Grace firmly, ignoring her son. 'I promised her that she'd have a dress to be married in.'

'Is she getting married, then?' asked Eliza excitedly. 'Who are you getting married to, Alys? Is it Francis?'

Alys blushed deeply. She saw her father and mother exchange glances.

'You can help me choose the dress, Eliza,' she said quickly.

'Let's cut the seal,' said Grace, producing a small sharp knife from the deep pocket that she wore tied around her waist.

She scored the wax seal on the chest, and Niall lifted the lid. Eliza gasped with astonishment. The last time the chest had been opened she had been too young to take much interest in the dresses, but now they filled her with excitement.

One by one the dresses were taken out – purple velvet, green silk, royal–blue satin; a white brocade trimmed with crimson; a cream silk kirtle embroidered with pale pink roses, with a farthingale of deep rose velvet – and spread over the bed. Last of all came a pale primrose-coloured silk dress. It was simpler than the others, but to Alys's eye it was the most beautiful of all.

'I'll have this one, Granny, if I may,' she said, holding the dress up against herself and spinning around so that the wide skirt flowed and swirled.

'It looks very old-fashioned,' sniffed Donogh.

'You look beautiful,' said Niall heartily.

'And when you are fourteen, Eliza,' said Grace, 'the chest will be opened again and you can pick out a dress for your wedding day.'

'I'll have the blue one,' said Eliza happily.

'Now let's seal it up again,' said Niall, 'and get it into the hidey-hole, and then I'll attach the clothes press in front of the opening. I'll loosen one board; if you ever see anyone coming, Donogh, just pull that board out, climb in, and pull the board back. No one will ever suspect that there's a space behind the press.'

'And I'll hang all my clothes up in the press. Then they'll never notice the loose board at the back,' said Alys.

The press was finished that evening. The next after-noon, they were all hard at work limewashing the cottage when Eliza, who had been outside collecting eggs, yelled,

'There are some people coming! They're riding up the avenue.'

'It's probably nothing,' said Niall, 'but in you get, Donogh. Don't worry; no one will know you're there. Just sit on the chest and wait until one of us calls you.'

In a flash Donogh was in the clothes press. Alys and her father watched as he wrenched out the loose board, climbed through into the secret space and then clicked the board back into place. It had all taken less than a minute, and he had done it all by himself. Niall nodded with satisfaction and looked around the white walls of the little bedroom, comparing them with the newly built walls around the hiding-place.

'No one could tell the difference,' said Alys. 'Those walls look as if they'd been there forever.'

'Let's go downstairs,' said Niall. 'The limewash is fresh — but then, Dermot is doing the kitchen and your mother is doing our bedroom, so no one could suspect anything strange about us doing the loft bedroom as well.'

They climbed down the ladder, carrying the bucket of limewash. Eliza was just coming in the door, panting.

'Alys,' she said, 'it's Francis! He's riding up the avenue, and he has a sword and a pistol! And there are two men with him — I don't know who they are. One of them is tall and thin, and the other one's short and fat. They're both wearing big black cloaks with hoods over their faces.'

Chapter Thirteen

'Oh, is it Francis?' said Betty, coming out of the east bedroom. 'Run upstairs, Dermot, and tell Donogh that it's all right.'

'No, stop,' said Alys. She hadn't told her mother about her doubts about Francis, but she had to be sure of him before she betrayed Donogh's hiding-place. 'He's got two other men with him,' she continued hastily. 'We don't know who they might be. I'll go and talk to them.'

Pulling her red cloak from the nail in the back door, she ran down the avenue. The snow had gone, and a sullen, heavy mist was drenching everything. The murky greens and browns of the fields and the hedgerows made Alys feel as if there would never be sun again.

The three horsemen had dismounted and were walking slowly up the avenue, leading their horses. Francis looked pale – Alys noticed that even from a

distance – and he walked heavily, but otherwise he seemed to have recovered. Her heart gave a great bound of joy. So he didn't have the plague; Michael had been right, it was just the Irish ague.

Who were the other two men, though? Alys stared at them, puzzled. There was something familiar about both of them, especially the small fat one. Those weather-beaten cheeks, the bold black eyes, the small tight mouth . . . of course!

'Máire Rua!' gasped Alys.

'Máire Rua it is,' said that lady, putting back her hood. She was wearing a pair of man's breeches, a shirt and a doublet, with a heavy dark cloak covering everything.

The tall thin man put back his hood as well, and Alys saw the tired, lined face of Father Dominic.

'How are you, child?' he said, putting his hand on her head and murmuring a blessing.

'Where's Donogh?' put in Máire Rua quickly. 'Those Cromwellian soldiers have been to every O'Brien house in the neighbourhood, even over to my first husband's place at Dysert O'Dea, but there's not been a sign of him.'

Alys glanced around. They were a long way from the road, but caution had grown in her during the past week.

'He's here,' she said briefly.

'Good girl,' said Máire Rua with satisfaction. 'I knew I could rely on you. You remind me of myself when I was young.'

And you were married at my age, thought Alys, stealing a glance at Francis. He was more handsome than ever, she thought. The slight pallor made him look noble and interesting. His hair had been cut, she noticed; he no longer had the flowing locks of a Royalist, though he wasn't wearing the clipped pudding-basin cut of many Cromwellians. A slight chill came over her. Where did Francis stand? Was he loyal to the Royalist cause, or did he follow his stepfather in thinking that the only hope lay in joining Cromwell?

'You two men go on up to the house,' ordered Máire Rua. 'Alys will stay with me. I'll have to give a breather to this poor old broken-down animal of Michael's. I didn't dare ride Chancer; those Cromwellians might have known me if I had. As it was, I managed to steal out the back entrance. I'm supposed to be resting on my bed at the moment.'

She gave a throaty chuckle, and Alys looked at her in amazement. Nothing daunts this woman's spirit, she thought. After all that's happened to her in the last week – the death of her two little daughters and the slaughter of her husband – she's still her bold self, ready to take on the world.

'Go on, you two,' Máire Rua repeated. 'I want to talk to Alys.'

In silence, Francis and Father Dominic walked up the avenue, and in silence Alys looked after them. Francis hadn't looked at her, hadn't greeted her. Was that guilt?

Did he suspect that she knew what had really happened to Conor O'Brien?

'Francis is going to France, to join Lord Inchiquin and the other Royalists in Paris,' said Máire Rua, following the direction of her gaze. 'I'll lend him the money. He's going to take Father Dominic with him. And I want . . .' Her voice broke a little, and she tightened her mouth. 'I want him to take Donogh, too. Lord Inchiquin is my husband's cousin; he'll look after Donogh. He won't be safe in Ireland while Cromwell's in charge. There's no hope for any of us now. We're going to lose our lands – most of them, anyway. They're going to drive all the Catholics from the rich lands of Cork and Tipperary, into Clare. Your father may lose all, or almost all, of his hundred acres, you know. We're all going to suffer, small landowners as well as large.'

'Yes,' said Alys. I can't take any more trouble and suffering, she thought.

Máire Rua looked at her closely. 'Tell me about Conor's death,' she said softly.

'Sir Charles and Colonel Roberts were traitors,' said Alys slowly. 'They betrayed your husband. They were lying in wait for him at Inchicronan. I went to warn him, but I couldn't save him. He went to help John – he could have saved himself, but he went to help John – and they shot him. He was fatally wounded.' She stopped and swallowed hard. I must be brave, she thought. If Máire Rua can listen without a tear, then I can tell her without sobbing.

'Conor said to send you all his love,' she went on steadily. 'He said you were the best wife a man could ever have.' She stole a glance at Máire Rua's face. The sloe-black eyes were opaque, as if a shutter had been drawn down to hide her thoughts. The weather-beaten cheeks were wet; but they were wet with rain. Máire Rua's eyes remained dry, and her mouth did not quiver.

'He was only twenty-one when I married him, you know,' she said abruptly after a minute. 'I never really imagined him growing old.' Her face was bleak and bitter.

'Then he said . . . he said to save his son,' faltered Alys.

The black eyes suddenly snapped back to life. 'I'll do that, if I have to marry Oliver Cromwell himself,' said Máire Rua, and her hearty laugh boomed out. 'I have to think of them all,' she added. 'There's my three Neylon sons – William will soon be finishing his fosterage, and I'll have to try to safeguard his inheritance. But Donogh's the one that the Cromwellians are after. They wormed it out of Torlach that there was a nursemaid and that Donogh might be with her. Luckily the little chatterbox couldn't describe very clearly where you lived, and I pretended that Macha was the nursemaid, but it won't take them too long to pick up the trail to here. Francis will have to take Donogh away tonight, after midnight.'

'Are you sure you can trust Francis?' faltered Alys. 'Mightn't he go to the Cromwellians' side with his stepfather? Whose side is he on?'

Máire Rua gave her a long, considering look. Then she turned away and began to plod up the steep avenue, holding the bridle of Michael's horse in her hand. After a few steps, she paused and looked over her shoulder.

'Why don't you ask him?' she said blandly. 'You're a woman now. You must make up your own mind about people. No one else can do that for you.'

She's right, thought Alys. I have to make up my mind about Francis. I don't suppose I'll ever see him again if he's going to France tonight, but I must know. And I must give him Sir Charles's message and that purse of gold.

Quickly she gathered up her trailing skirt and began to run up the avenue. In a few seconds she overtook Máire Rua and passed her without a glance. She had to see Francis, had to talk to him before Máire Rua said anything in front of him.

She rushed into the little kitchen. There was no sign of Donogh; he must still be hidden upstairs. Father Dominic sat on the best chair by the fire, talking in low tones to Betty and Grace; Francis was standing by the north window, gloomily looking out at the rain. Alys crossed the room and touched his arm.

'Come for a walk down to the river with me,' she said quickly.

'What? In the rain?' asked her mother in amazement.

'Let her go,' said Grace quietly.

Without a word, Francis followed her out.

Neither of them spoke on their way down to the river. From time to time, Alys stole a glance at Francis and found that he was looking at her too; when their eyes met, they both flushed and looked away.

When they reached the river, Alys kept her eyes fixed intently on the fast-flowing brown water and waited for Francis to speak. He said nothing, however, so she had to break the silence.

'Do you know how Conor O'Brien died? Do you know who betrayed him?' Her voice was harsh and dry.

'I can guess,' he answered in a dull voice.

'Did you know beforehand?' she asked abruptly. 'Did you know what was planned?'

Francis didn't answer. He was staring into the river, the toe of his boot scuffing the dried stalks of the water mint that grew on the bank. His face looked very young and ashamed, Alys thought.

'Did you know?' she asked again, more gently this time.

He cleared his throat, but his voice was still husky and strained.

'I wasn't sure,' he said. He stopped and then went on, 'I wasn't sure. I heard things, but I was never really certain. . . . The first night we came to Lemeanah, I thought I heard – heard them saying something, on the road; but I told myself I was wrong. And Smith – Cornet Smith – sometimes he'd be away for a day or two, and none of the men would know where he'd gone. Now I know, of course – I know he must have been taking information about our side to the Cromwellians, and bringing back instructions for the Colonel and my – my stepfather. But I just – I just thought Smith must be taking messages to other regiments and reporting back to Colonel Roberts. I suppose I fooled myself. He – Sir Charles – has been good to me, you know; and my mother is very fond of him. I didn't want to make trouble, so I just pretended to myself that I'd made a mistake.'

'So did I,' said Alys softly. She put her hand on his. 'I overheard things too, things that should have made me suspicious; but I told myself that it was nothing to do with me. I told myself I was mistaken.'

Francis met her glance for the first time. His brown eyes were full of trouble. 'It's worse for me,' he said. 'I'm supposed to be a soldier. But who could I talk to? Colonel Roberts was my commanding officer. I should have talked to Conor O'Brien, though. I wonder if he would have believed me.'

'And I should have talked to Máire Rua,' said Alys. 'I wonder if she would have believed *me*.'

There was a pause. A deep sadness seemed to overwhelm them both. The rain continued to fall, a thick mist that soaked through their hoods. Alys felt her eyelashes fringed with drops of moisture.

'And now you're going away,' she said sadly.

'I'm going away,' Francis repeated. There was another silence. Then, with a visible effort, he forced himself to speak again.

'I'm going to join the king in France,' he explained. 'At least that's something I can do. And I can save Conor O'Brien's son. I've sworn to Máire Rua that I will defend him with my life. I won't fail this time.'

'So we'll never see each other again after tonight,' said Alys.

'No, I suppose not,' he said sombrely.

She turned to go away, to go back to the house. Then she remembered.

'Sir Charles gave me a purse of gold for you,' she said, taking the purse from her pocket and turning back to Francis.

'I don't want it,' he said in a muffled voice, his face turned away from her. 'I don't want anything from him. I'll steer my own course from now on.'

Alys took a step back and looked closely at him. He was crying. Suddenly she saw him as a boy, a boy not much older than herself. He had made a mistake – had not been as brave, perhaps, as he felt he should have been – but so had she. In the future they would have each other for comfort and for advice.

'Take it,' she said firmly. 'You'll need it if you have a wife.'

Suddenly Francis's face blazed with excitement. His brown eyes looked at her tenderly.

'Alys, you don't mean . . . you couldn't . . . would you, after all?' he said, the words tumbling over each other.

I do mean it, thought Alys. I know it won't be easy – I'll be far from home, from Drumshee, from my parents. But I love Francis and I want to be with him for the rest of my life. Máire Rua is right: I'm a woman now. I must decide for myself.

She moved closer to Francis and smiled up at him.

'If you ask me properly,' she said.

He didn't really ask her, but the kiss that followed was enough to satisfy her. And when eventually they wandered back up through the meadow, hand in hand, there were no questions or answers between them – just plans for the future.

Chapter Fourteen

Alys had often dreamed of her wedding day, especially since the night of the Hallowe'en party. It would be in the little church down the road from Drumshee, of course. Everyone would be there – family, aunts and uncles and cousins, friends and neighbours. She had even planned the flowers in the church.

But there was no church, no altar, no guests and no flowers. There was a priest, though. Father Dominic was to perform the ceremony that night, in the kitchen of Drumshee. Máire Rua was a witness – and without her there might have been no wedding.

'Francis is a good lad; my Conor thought very well of him,' she said. 'Alys will be safe with him. And she'll be better off out of this country; there are darker days ahead. She can make her home in France, or in England when King Charles, God bless him, gets back his throne.

There will always be a place for the younger ones to go to – even for yourselves, if things get too bad.'

'Let her go,' said Grace. 'Cecilia went at that age. She's lucky she's found someone to love, someone who loves her. Parents have to give up their children at some stage. Alys knows her own mind.'

And so Betty and Niall had to agree. Betty hastily made a cake on the griddle over the fire. All the family changed into their best clothes, and Alys wore the dress of primrose-coloured silk that had come from her grandmother's chest.

Standing in front of the wooden dresser that her grandfather had made, Alys bowed her head as Father Dominic blessed her and Francis and sprinkled them both with holy water. Then Máire Rua took a gold ring from her own finger and handed it to Father Dominic, who blessed it and gave it to Francis. Francis slipped it onto Alys's finger.

'With this ring I thee wed,' said Father Dominic.

'With this ring I thee wed,' repeated Francis.

'And I plight unto thee my troth.'

'And I plight unto thee my troth,' said Francis, his voice firm and steady.

And then it was all over. Francis kissed Alys; then her father and mother, her grandmother, her brother and sister, even Máire Rua, kissed her. There were tears and laughter. There were cakes and ale. Everyone – even Donogh – was eating and drinking and laughing as if there were no dark shadow over the land of Ireland.

'We might even come out to France and join you, someday, if things get too bad,' said Betty; but Niall shook his head silently. Alys knew that her father would never leave Drumshee. He would hold the land, keep it as safe as he could; and then it would be Dermot's turn, and then Dermot's children, and so on down through the ages.

'Time for you four to get going now,' said Máire Rua, in a severely practical voice. Alys stole a glance at her. Once more the black eyes were shuttered, all feeling safely hidden behind them. Máire Rua would suffer terribly at the parting from her beloved son, but no one would be allowed to guess at that suffering.

'Come on, Donogh, we'd better cut your hair,' she continued. 'It would never do for you to look like a little Cavalier. Alys, you could trim Francis's hair some more, as well. It's still a bit too long.'

Donogh didn't make as much fuss as Alys had expected at having his flowing ringlets cut off – probably the sight of Francis being clipped by Alys made him feel better. But he gave a cry of protest when Betty said thoughtfully, 'Wouldn't it be better to disguise him as a girl? The word may have gone out to watch for a nine-year-old boy. We could easily put him into Eliza's outgrown dress.'

She couldn't have used a worse word than 'outgrown', thought Alys with amusement. Donogh was very conscious of his own dignity, but he was even more conscious of his lack of height.

'No,' he said violently. 'I'm not dressing up in that girl's clothes.'

Máire Rua looked at him steadily. 'You're the *taoiseach* now, Donogh,' she said softly. 'Your clan will be relying on you. You must keep yourself safe and come back to lead your kin into battle.'

Suddenly Donogh seemed to grow taller before their eyes. He looked at his mother, and it was as if some of her spirit and courage flowed into him.

'Whatever you think is best, Mother,' he said with dignity.

'Dermot, you come upstairs and help me with Alys's bag,' said Niall quickly. The beginnings of a grin were coming over Dermot's face, but Alys and Niall quickly got him up the ladder before his chuckle broke out.

'He didn't need to have his pretty curls cut off, after all, if he's going to be a girl,' Dermot grinned when they were in Alys's bedroom; but he said it in a low voice, and Alys was sure that Donogh wouldn't be able to hear. In any case, there were no further cries of protest from the kitchen below.

'You can have this leather bag,' said Niall, pulling something down from under the thatch. 'It used to belong to your grandmother. The catch is gone from it, but I've got a piece of rope that we can tie it with; that should stop it opening.'

'I wish I could take the yellow dress,' said Alys longingly, 'but there'll be no room for it. I'll leave it in the press until I come home again.'

Somehow the act of hanging the primrose-coloured dress in the clothes press made it seem more likely that she would, someday, come home again. Suddenly Alys felt excited, full of energy and hope for the future.

By the time they got downstairs again, Donogh was dressed in Eliza's old clothes, and Máire Rua was making an artistic job of tousling his hair into a mass of tangles.

'Time you were on your way,' she said, ushering them all out of the kitchen and into the dark cold of the farm-yard. At the doorstep she bent down, dipped her finger in a puddle and smeared some mud on Donogh's cheeks.

'There,' she said. 'You can ride in front of Father Dominic. Now no one will ever guess that you're The O'Brien of Lemeanah.'

Donogh visibly swelled with pride and allowed his mother to lift him onto Father Dominic's horse.

'You have a great night for the ride,' said Grace. 'The rain has stopped and the moon's coming out from the clouds. You'll see your way well; you'll have no need for a lantern.'

'I'll be home soon,' said Alys. Her mother's eyes were wet with tears, but her grandmother's dry eyes seemed even sadder.

'Please God,' said Grace. 'God bless you, my child. Be happy.'

'Here's Silky,' said Dermot. 'I've tacked her up for you.'

Francis lifted Alys into the saddle and then swung himself onto Sultan's back.

'Francis, have you enough money?' enquired Máire Rua, taking out her purse.

'Yes, I have. You've given me more than enough. Oh, I forgot — I've also got a purse from . . . from my step-father. I don't know what's in it, though.'

Máire Rua's face darkened, but her voice didn't change. 'Well, open it, lad,' she said. 'See how much he's sent you.'

'Twenty pieces of gold,' said Francis, counting it.

'Twenty pieces of gold!' exclaimed Betty. 'Well, you'll want for nothing with that.'

'There's a piece of paper, too,' said Eliza, bending down and picking something up off the ground. 'Look, Francis, this fell out of the purse.'

Niall brought the lantern over and held it high while Francis read aloud.

Allow to pass in safety Cornet Francis Chandler, stepson of Sir Charles Cunningham.
Signed:
Henry Ireton
Limerick

'He must have persuaded Ireton that you were on the Cromwellian side,' said Máire Rua. 'I suppose that would have been easy enough. After all, you're only seventeen — most seventeen-year-olds would follow where their stepfather led.'

That's true, thought Alys. It's very brave of Francis to think for himself and cut himself loose from his stepfather. She moved nearer to him and took his hand in hers.

'Keep that,' commanded Máire Rua. 'It may be useful to you. Go now,' she added, her voice high and harsh. 'Do as Lord Inchiquin tells you, Donogh, and come back a soldier.' Then she turned and walked back into the house.

'God bless you all,' said Niall. 'God keep you safe.'

'Goodbye,' said Alys steadily. 'I'll write to you when I can.'

And then they were on their way, riding down the avenue and through the gate that Dermot held open. Alys paused for a moment when she was through the gate. She looked back at the hillside, the little cottage where she had been born, the old fort looming above it, the river gurgling at the bottom of the hill.

'Goodbye, Drumshee,' she said under her breath. Then she turned Silky's head towards the west. By morning they would be at Liscannor.

It was an easy journey, as Grace had predicted. For once the sky was bare of clouds, and the full moon made everything as bright as day. They rode steadily; there was no rush now. The ship wouldn't leave before dawn, and in these dark days dawn didn't come before eight o'clock. At first, from time to time, a muffled sob escaped Donogh; but Father Dominic chatted gently and cheerfully to him all the way, and by the time they reached Lickeen Lake, Donogh was beginning to reply.

'I'll teach you French on the voyage,' promised Father Dominic. 'We'll start now. *"Bonjour"* is the French for "good day".'

'*Bonjour*,' repeated Donogh, and Alys was heartened to hear a slight chuckle in his voice. Donogh will be all right, she thought. He had grown up immensely in the last few days; he wasn't the spoilt, demanding little boy she had first met. Someday he would be a soldier like his father, though perhaps never as merry and open-hearted as Conor had been.

It's Francis I'm worried about, she thought. He still looked very different from the carefree boy he had been on Hallowe'en night. He rode in silence, his face lowered, his eyes dark and unsmiling. He's still ashamed, thought Alys. Every time he looks at Donogh, or at Máire Rua, he remembers Conor's death and he starts thinking about how he could, perhaps, have saved him. Alys knew how he felt – she felt rather like that herself – but she guessed that it must be worse for Francis: he had been brought up to be a soldier, to value courage and loyalty above everything else.

The clock in the stableyard at Smithstown was chiming when they passed. Alys listened, counting the strokes.

'Five o'clock,' she said with satisfaction. 'We're making good time.'

'What's that?' asked Francis, alarm in his voice.

Alys listened. At first she hoped that she was mistaken; but soon she knew she wasn't. A party of men were riding rapidly towards them. She looked around, but there was no place to hide. This land had no hedges, no large trees; even the stone walls were low, too low for anyone to hide behind.

'Wait,' whispered Francis. 'Stop. Alys, give me that rope from your bag.'

Bewildered, Alys untied the rope and handed it to him.

'Hold out your hands, Father,' Francis commanded. Quickly he tied the priest's hands in front of him, looped the rope around Donogh's hands as well, and then tied Alys's hands together with one end and held the other end himself.

'Don't say a word,' he hissed. 'Leave all the talking to me. If they ask you anything, just mutter something in Irish.'

A moment later, the men came into sight. They were a small party of soldiers, dressed in full armour, and one glance at their cropped hair told Alys that they were Cromwellians. Her heart sank.

'Halt,' shouted the captain.

Francis saluted him. 'Cornet Francis Chandler, at your service,' he said smartly. 'I've been detailed to take this man and his two granddaughters to Ennistymon for questioning. Here's my pass.' He reached into his pocket, found the pass Sir Charles had sent him, and handed it to the captain.

Alys felt her hands wet with sweat. Would it work? The name on the pass – Ireton – was familiar to her, for some reason. Where had she heard it before?

Suddenly her mind cleared. It was Donogh who had said it, in the kitchen at Lemeanah – she could hear the clear, childish voice. 'Ireton,' Donogh had said. 'He's Cromwell's son-in-law.' Alys's hands suddenly felt warmer. Surely the soldiers would take notice of a pass signed by Cromwell's son-in-law?

They did! The captain was saluting Francis, Francis was saluting him, and they jogged on.

'Ride slowly, keep your heads down and look depressed,' whispered Francis.

After a few minutes, Alys dared to look back. There was no sign of the Cromwellians.

'They're gone,' said Father Dominic at the same moment.

'We'd better keep the rope on, though,' said Donogh in a low voice. 'They might come back.'

'Clever boy,' said Alys.

'What do you mean, *boy*?' said Francis, with a laugh. 'That's a young lady there in front of Father Dominic.'

Donogh giggled. 'Was I a good girl?' he demanded.

'Perfect,' Francis assured him.

Alys looked at him. He sounded like the old Francis, full of fun and confidence. His face, too, looked more normal, from what she could see. By the white light of the moon, she could see a sparkle in his brown eyes, and there was a flash of white teeth from behind the golden beard and moustache. Francis held his head high – and suddenly Alys understood. His quick thinking had saved them all, had saved Conor O'Brien's son; he was no longer so ashamed of himself.

'I don't know how you managed to think of that plan so quickly,' she said softly, thinking how handsome he looked, and how young. He would look after her, she knew, but she would also look after him. They would be very happy together.

Dawn was breaking as they came down the hill from Kilshanny. In front of them were the bay of Liscannor, a great crescent of golden sand at Lahinch, and a small port in Liscannor village. Anchored at the port was a large ship, its sails gleaming white in the brightening sky.

'Quick,' said Francis, untying the rope from the others' wrists. 'Ride quickly. She looks ready to cast off.'

They almost flew down the hill – Francis first on Sultan, then Silky with her blond mane streaming back in the west wind, then Father Dominic with Donogh, all of them thundering along, going as fast as they could.

The ship's captain was happy to have them on board, once he saw the gold coin Francis offered him. There were two fine cabins for them, one for Francis and Alys and the other for Father Dominic and Donogh; there was good stabling for the three horses below deck, and there would be plenty of provisions for all.

Father Dominic went down to his cabin while Francis, Alys and Donogh saw to the horses. By the time they came back up on deck, the ship had weighed anchor and was well out from the shore.

Alys stood in the bows of the ship, holding her husband Francis's large warm hand in one of her own and Donogh's small cold hand in the other. She stood there, watching the sunrise – first a fiery red ball coming up over the hills, and then a golden sun whose faint heat warmed their faces.

The dark days are over, she thought. From now on, I'll be in the sun.

Author's Note

Conor O'Brien, Máire Rua O'Brien and their children were all real people. When Máire Rua was fourteen or fifteen, she was married to Daniel Neylon of Dysert, near Corofin. They had three sons, William, Daniel and Michael. Daniel Neylon died in March 1639; in October 1639, Máire Rua married Conor O'Brien and moved to Lemeanah Castle, leaving her three Neylon sons to be fostered by the Carrigy family.

Máire Rua and Conor O'Brien had eight children, of whom six survived infancy: Donogh (born in 1641), Teige, Torlach, Honora (born in 1645), Mary and Slaney. Mary and Slaney both died in 1651, the same year that their father was killed at Inchicronan Pass. There is a memorial plaque to the two little girls in Coad Church, and in a way it gave rise to the story of this book.

The ruins of Lemeanah Castle – both the old tower and the magnificent mansion built by Máire Rua and Conor O'Brien – can still be seen on the road between Corofin and Kilfenora.

HERE LYES THE
BODIES OF MARY AND
SLANY NY BRIENDAVGH
TERS TO CONNOROBRIEN
AND MARY BRIEN ALIAS
MAHON OFLEMINEACH
ANND OMINI 1651

CAVAN COUNTY LIBRARY

COMING SOON ...

Book 13
in the gripping
Drumshee Timeline Series:

The Secret Spy from Drumshee

'Daniel O'Connell is in deadly danger and you must be the secret spy from Drumshee,' says Mary Ann to her brother Ronan. 'You don't talk much, so no one will notice you.'

Sharp-eyed and intelligent, Ronan watches and listens.

But Mary Ann doesn't realise that the task she has given her crippled and almost wordless brother will put his life in deadly danger.

Plunge into the dark events of 1825 in book 13 of the Drumshee Timeline series. Daniel O'Connell is fighting for a new way of life for the Irish people but there are enemies on every side. With Mary Ann's help, Ronan tries to save Daniel O'Connell. But can Ronan save this Irish hero from an evil assassin?